A Ring Of Rejoicement

Naomi Sharp

DEDICATION

I dedicate this book to Mr Countryside. You have opened
my heart to receive life's greatest gifts. You've inspired
and guided. Yet, most of all, you have left footprints on
my heart and showed me that any dream can come true.

CONTENTS

1 A PLACE TO CALL HOME

Ally's footsteps chimed on the wooden steps as she walked up to the front door. Her heart was beating fast. Not with fear of what lay behind that door, but with pure excitement. Excitement about the memories which protect and nurture: her very own treasure box.

As she stepped closer, the overhang of the front porch cast a shadow over her. Her fingers slowly curled around the handle, and turned it. She gave the door a single push and it swung wide open. She paused a moment and allowed a familiar feeling to wash over her body, as she was catapulted back to the very first time she had seen the house. A pool of sunlight created a perfect picture frame of the vast countryside, as it streamed through the large, floor-to-ceiling glass windows.

Ally's gaze drifted to the right and settled on the large, stone fireplace and the cosy sofas in front. She remembered the nights when she and Ben would watch a movie, as she rested her head comfortably on his shoulder. She turned to look at the office door which led into a space that always seemed to magnify ideas: a safe place to take bold action.

Ally took a deep breath in. The house always felt warm, as if it had absorbed and filled itself with every bit of the day's sunlight. Her nostrils filled with the smell of fresh coffee and she tuned into the sound of bubbles from the boiling kettle. She glanced across at the large, wooden kitchen table. Each scratch carved into the surface symbolised a memory of fun and laughter. A shot of bliss ran up from her toes all the way up to the tip of her nose. '*This is a place I can call home*,' she thought.

The silence of her thoughts was suddenly broken. "Ben, you best come and help Mom. She seems to have become a statue," called Hugh as he tilted his head to the side and surveyed his mom, paused in the front doorway. Ben poked his head out from the truck as he lifted Molly's suitcase out. "Hang on, Buddy. I'll be with you in a minute," he replied. "There you go, little Miss," he said, handing the suitcase to Molly.

2

Ben picked up his case and made his way towards Ally. Ally listened to the familiar sound of his boots as they rang against the wood. Ben walked up the steps to the front door, and she waited, with anticipation, for this moment. He placed his hand gently on Ally's back as he leaned towards her. "Welcome home, Miss Ally," he whispered. Ally took hold of Ben's hand, as together, they stepped over the threshold, into their life. The life that they were creating together.

Molly and Hugh filed in behind. "It's good to be home," Hugh called, and his words echoed around the living room. He ran across and jumped into the sofa. His body melted into the softness of the cushions, and he let out a deep sigh. Molly walked awkwardly into the kitchen. She reached for the kettle, unsure of where she belonged in this web of love.

At that moment, Billy stepped out of the office. "Welcome home, Son," he said, striding across to where they were all standing. "So, I guess it all went well?" he enquired as he took a step back to better scan their faces.
"Yes, all sorted," answered Ben. "But, what about here?" he asked nervously.
"Well, the coffee is fresh," replied Billy. "Why don't we grab a cup and I'll fill you in," he added as he walked into the kitchen.

Billy watched Molly as she precariously balanced on her tip toes, trying to reach a cup. He stepped through and passed one to her. "You'll find your boxes waiting for you in your room," he said softly. Molly thrust the cup back at him and ran towards her room. Ally peeled off her coat and threw it on top of Hugh, who was still laid out on the sofa. "Hey!" he called with a big grin.

Ally began to make herself a cup of tea. Ben took his usual seat at the end of the kitchen table and Billy passed him a much-needed cup of coffee. Molly bounded down the stairs, carefully carrying Nana O's teapot and a cup. When she reached the kitchen, she placed them down by the kettle and Ally began, robotically, to fill it full of hot water. "Good idea," she muttered. Molly filled her cup with fresh tea and milk before disappearing back up to her new room. Hugh popped his head up to watch Molly climb the stairs. He then sluggishly rolled his body off the sofa and followed her.

Ally joined Ben and Billy at the kitchen table and wrapped her hands around the warm mug. "Well, there isn't really much to report," said Billy. "The animals are all doing well. Tom and I have been fixing the fences on some of the pastures and the house didn't burn down. So, I would say it's gone pretty well!" he added in jest.

4

Ben lifted his cap, placed it on the table in front of him and ran his hands through his hair. "Good, that's good," he said distantly.

Billy gave him a worried glance. "And I have just been updating all the figures on your spread sheets," he said. Ben shot him a '*don't say anymore,*' warning look.

Ally watched intently at the conversation that wasn't being spoken between them. "Well, I am going to head into town with the kids, and get Molly set up in her room," she declared. "And have a look if there are any jobs going," she added as she slurped her tea.

Ben looked across at Ally. "Let's just focus on getting you all set up and settled in," he soothed. "The ranch can support this family," he added decisively.

Ally raised her eyebrows in response. "In a matter of moments," she began. "Your family went from you and your animals, to four people and your animals! Unless there is a secret fortune you are sitting on that I don't know about, we will be needing all the help we can get."

Ben scrunched his eyebrows in pain. He knew that what Ally was saying was correct, but the pang of failure stung him like a broken string on his heart.

"Things will work out," said Ben as he got up

from the table. He grabbed his cup of coffee and headed upstairs to get changed. Billy watched Ben disappear, waiting until he was out of sight before he spoke. "I think that wouldn't be such a bad idea, Ally," he said. "Don't let Ben's pride deceive you. Now, what about Molly?' he asked. "Well, that little lady will never have to work a day in her life," replied Ally. "She is now known as Millionaire Molly! Ha! Actually," she corrected. "Make that Multimillionaire Molly! But, we have decided to put it in a trust until she is 30 years old. This will give her chance to be a child and make her mistakes without too much of a high price to pay."

Billy nodded at the idea. "Seems fair enough to me," he acknowledged. "But, how come she came into so much money?" he asked in confusion.

Ally stretched back in her chair and chuckled. She still marvelled at how a single moment could change everything. Such a miracle. "Nana O left her a cheque for £1.2 million to begin with," Ally explained. "Then with the house sale and the insurance, the total just tripled over night! The interest alone is enough to live on!" Ally said in wonderment. "Can you believe it?"

Billy shook his head. "That Nana of hers was a very clever woman!" he breathed. "She didn't listen to the gossip on the streets, but she always followed her gut feelings. And by the sounds of it, acting upon that guidance served her very well." Billy smiled as the memory of Nana O flashed through his mind.

Ben reappeared at the kitchen doorway in his jeans and shirt, his expression a little softer now. He walked into the kitchen and placed his empty cup by the side of the sink, and then reached into his pocket. He slid his bank card towards Ally. "Use this for Molly's things," he said. "I'll be saddling up and heading out with Tom, before he heads off." Ben kissed Ally on the top of her head, before heading towards the front door and slipping on his boots. As he stepped out of the front door Billy and Ally listened intently to the click of it closing. Ally continued to watch him walk towards the barn through the kitchen window.

Ally slowly picked the card up off the table and twirled it around in her fingers. She scowled. "This isn't going to happen again," she muttered decisively as she slid the card into her pocket. "I'll be contributing too," she said as she got up from the table. Billy raised his eyebrows but stayed silent. He knew that anything he said next would be the wrong thing.

Ally walked with determination across the wooden floor, towards the stairs. As she climbed each step, the sound of Molly and Hugh got louder. Ally slowly pushed Molly's bedroom door open. Molly was putting her blue dress on a hanger and placing it in her wardrobe. Hugh lay lazily on her bed with his feet resting against the wall. "How are you getting on?" Ally asked as she perched on the edge of the bed. Hugh sneakily shuffled closer and placed his head on Ally's lap. Ally instinctively began to play with his hair.

"Nearly all unpacked," answered Molly as she threw an empty box through the doorway and out onto the landing.

"Well, I was thinking that we best go into town to pick up a few things, to really make this room more your own," answered Ally. "You too, Hugh," she added. "Seeing as this is the place we are going to be calling home from now on."

Hugh glanced up at Ally. "Shouldn't we have brought our stuff from England then as well?" he enquired.

Ally winced. She knew he was right, but she just didn't have the strength to pack up another house at the moment. "Probably," she mumbled. It was the best response she could muster up. "We'll do that next time we're back."

Molly came and joined Ally and Hugh on the bed. She looked around the room, trying to imagine what she wanted. "Maybe a few picture frames and a lamp," she suggested. "Oh, and some new curtains would be great!" Molly finished, as the scene in her mind became clearer.

"Right then! Everyone to the truck!" Ally declared. She nearly knocked Hugh off the bed as she stood up. They all proceeded, single file, down the stairs. Billy was still sitting at the kitchen table. Ally noticed that his eyes looked weary and tired. "I think you had better get back to your place and put your feet up," she said lovingly. "You have definitely earnt it."

Billy smiled weakly. "It has been a bit of a shock to the body, to be honest," he confessed. "I forgot what it was like to run this place. It's a lot more efficient than when I had it, but there is always something to be done," he said as he got up from the table. Ally nodded her acknowledgement.

Hugh took hold of Ally's hand and he began to pull her towards the front door. "Come on, Mom," he urged. "It's time to go." Ally surrendered as she let Hugh lead her to the truck. Molly followed closely behind.

They all climbed into the truck, and Billy got into his. Billy pulled away first and he drove down the driveway. He glanced in the rear view mirror and saw Ben give a single wave of his hat, before the sight of Ally's truck filled his view.

Ben walked back into the barn with his hands pushed deep into his pockets. He walked over to Firefly, who was tied up outside her stable. Her saddle and bridle were already on, ready for the ride. He gently placed his hand on her hind quarters, and ran his fingertips through her soft hair. But, his gaze cast downwards. He took in a slow breath and felt the weight of reality weave a rope around his chest. As Tom entered the barn, he saw the solemn silhouette of Ben. "That is a big bag of troubles you've got there in your saddle bag," he said sympathetically.
Ben glanced at Tom, but wasn't able to force a smile. "Just some changes that need to be made," he answered heavily. "But, I just don't know where to start. There seems to be so much to do. And I can't find a starting thread on the end of this rope. So how will I begin threading a new life?"
Tom walked across and placed a hand on Ben's shoulder. "Well, doing nothing definitely isn't the answer," he declared. "It doesn't matter what you do though. Just do something, then let the momentum lead you onto the next step. Do what is in front of you and stop trying to change a whole life. Just change today," he finished wisely. "Now, come on. It has been a while since we have had a ride together."

Tom untied Red Rock, slipped his foot into the stirrup and climbed up onto the horse. Ben untied Firefly and did the same. "Well, if that's the case," said Ben, feeling a little brighter. "I had better assess the damage you've done, to see what I now need to repair," he said jokily. "Ha!" responded Tom in retaliation. "This ranch has never looked so good!" The two friends laughed as they alerted Firefly and Red Rock with a squeeze of their legs. The sound of horse hooves rang around the barn.

They steered the horses towards the gate and Ben reached down to swing it open. He felt his mind begin to settle as the scenery soothed his soul, once again. With each step he took, Ben imagined one of his troubles falling out of his saddle bag and onto the ground, for mother nature to do what she does best: transform them into something beautiful. Tom watched as the lines on Ben's face began to disappear. "Best medicine there is, nature," he mused. "It cures most problems, if you let it," he added wisely as he casually held the reins across his saddle horn. "You're not wrong there," smiled Ben in agreement.

The horses began to climb up the hill as they followed one of the paths made by the animals. Tom pointed out the work that he and Billy had

11

been doing whilst Ben had been away. Ben listened intently, as his gaze fell on the fencing, the new water system that had been built, and the repairs to one of the holding pens. He folded his arms and leant on his saddle horn. Firefly came to a stop as she reached the brow of the hill. The view suddenly opened up to a great expanse of breath-taking, beautiful countryside. Tom fell silent as they both became captivated by the enchanting view in front of them. "There are some places on this planet where Mother Nature puts on her grandest of shows," said Ben with uninhibited appreciation.

Tom slowed his horse to a stop alongside Ben. "Mate, we are the luckiest and richest people alive to have this piece of heaven to come to, whenever we want," he added gratefully.

Ben gently squeezed his legs against Firefly - a signal for her to continue. They made their way down the other side of the hill, towards the river. Each hoof print left a stamp of happiness on the land. Suddenly, something caught Ben's attention. He watched as a shadow moved at the other side of the river. He held his breath as the figure began to make its way towards the water's edge. The sunlight fell on the shadow and illuminated its golden, brown fur. A beautiful stag cautiously made its way. Its head turned left and right, surveying for danger, as it was joined by a deer and their grown fawn.

Ben smiled to himself. *It's been a while since I have seen you*, he thought. The memory of the day before he left for the country fair and rodeo, where he met Ally and Hugh for the first time, whooshed back into his mind. "What news do you bring me this time?" he pondered.
"Well, I'll be," whispered Tom as they continued to ride to the river's edge. The horses bent, gratefully, to take a drink. Tom playfully tapped Ben on the shoulder in approval. The stag and deer suddenly looked up, and they turned and leaped gracefully back into the cover of the trees.
"Come on," said Ben. "We best be looping back to the ranch, to make sure there isn't a truck arriving full of Ally, Hugh and Molly's shopping," he added cheekily.

"Last one there has to do evening chores," shouted Tom as he spun Red Rock around and started to canter back up the hill.
Ben slowly turned Firefly around. "He'll never learn," said Ben as he started on a different path back to the ranch.
As Red Rock began to fly, Tom pushed his hat further down on his head. "Come on, Red Rock! We've got it this time," he yelled excitedly as they leaped over the top of the hill and continued to canter down the other side. Tom's heart beat

quickened as the gate came into view. "No way!" he said in confusion. "It's not possible." He slowed Red Rock back to a trot and glared at the figure on horseback, already opening the gate. Ben stood, casually holding the gate as Tom slowed to walk. Tom shook his head as he passed Ben. "After you," invited Ben smugly.

They both began to laugh as they rode back towards the barn. But, their laughter was soon drowned out by the sound of the returning truck. Ben slowly dismounted as Tom took hold of the reins. "I had better be making a start on those evening chores," Tom said with a hint of disappointment.
"I'll be back in a minute, to help you out," Ben said reassuringly. But his focus honed in on the boot of the truck, which was stacked with bags.

Ally stepped out of the truck and Ben noticed the dark shadows beginning to form under her eyes. "Successful trip?" he asked as he opened up the boot.
Hugh and Molly sprang out of the truck and both began to grab the handles of each bag. "I can't wait to show you!" Hugh said excitedly as he and Molly waddled up the steps under the weight of the bags, and disappeared inside.
Ally appeared next and kissed Ben on the cheek. "I am never doing that again!" she said

determinedly. "There isn't enough tea in the country to make me want to shop like that!" Ben smiled sympathetically before heaving the remaining bags out the back. Ally followed and tiredly grabbed the last few.

They both made their way inside. Hugh slid across the living room floor, on his socks, and took some of the bags from Ben. Molly quickly followed suit and took the rest. Ally lowered hers to the ground and she made a beeline for the kettle. "Whatever you do," shouted Hugh. "Don't come upstairs! We want it to be a surprise," he explained as Molly giggled.

As the kettle began to boil, Ally emptied the contents of her handbag onto the table. It was mostly receipts and some local ads. Ben poured himself another coffee and sat down at the table. He slid the ads towards him. "Shop Assistant, Post Assistant, Home Help," he read aloud. He took a slow sip of coffee. "I know I've never asked this, but what did you do before Hugh's dad died? Did you work?" he asked carefully.
Ben looked up to see Ally glaring at him. "Yes!" she replied angrily. "I worked!"
"Hey," replied Ben. "Don't take offence. Being a mom is a full-time job."
"Don't I know it!" Ally replied defensively. "I used to organise events and promotions for a

company, and I was good at it too," Ally eventually explained. "But after Hugh's dad passed, I just couldn't piece myself back together, or face everyone and their questions, and them looking at me with pity. I know they weren't doing it to be unkind, but people never quite look at you in the same way again. I don't know, it's hard to put into words. I was planning to start looking for work again when Hugh and I got back from our trip. But you, kindly, sent my life spinning in a whole new direction."

Ally joined Ben at the table. "At the moment," she said. "I am not looking for anything specific. Just something, so that I can add to our pot of gold as well."
Ben scowled. He hated the thought of Ally not being able to be herself. He leant forwards on his elbows and looked deep into her eyes. "Miss Ally," he said tenderly. "Before you go whirling into something that is, ultimately, going to make you unhappy, how about you write down the job you have always wanted and dreamed of? Even if that job is just staying here looking after Molly and Hugh. We can only spend our time once. Make sure you spend it wisely, making memories, and on something that inspires and challenges you. It's just as important to live your own life and have your own aspirations, as it is to be part of this family."

Ally paused a moment, a little taken aback by Ben's words. "Of all people, I guess I should be the one to appreciate just how precious our time is," she pondered. "OK, I'll think on it." She reached across and squeezed Ben's hand.
They were suddenly interrupted by a breathless Molly who appeared in the kitchen doorway.
"Please could I borrow a screw driver and a hammer?" she asked, looking at Ben.
Ally's expression of bewilderment caught Molly's attention.
"Yes, of course," answered Ben. "There's a small tool kit under the sink. It should have everything you need." Molly darted across and retrieved the tool kit before dashing out of the kitchen and back up the stairs.

Ally couldn't hide a look of disapproval. "Do you think she should really be let loose with a hammer in your house?" she asked in concern.
"How else is she going to learn if she doesn't have the opportunity to try?" asked Ben. "And, there is no better place to learn these skills than in the safety of OUR house, under our watchful gaze," he added to strengthen his point.
Ally's expression softened. "Old habit," she said with a shrug.
"I hope you bought a few things on your shopping trip as well," questioned Ben. "You know, to make this place feel like your home as well," he said as

he got up from the table. "Right, I best go and help Tom with evening chores," he said as he walked around the back of Ally and wrapped his arms around her. "You are what makes this place a home," he added lovingly before making his way out of the front door.

Ally got up to make herself another cup of tea. She tried to soothe her nerves as she listened to the tap of the hammer in the rooms above, and Hugh shouting instructions to Molly. Ally let her head rest on the kitchen cupboard as a wash of relief flooded through her body. *We made it through*, she thought as her mind became silent. No more rushing around, no more job lists or phone calls to make, just a chance to slow everything down and catch her breath.

But, she suddenly winced as she heard a large thud upstairs and a voice very similar to Hugh's. "Agh!" he cried.
Ally peeled herself off the cupboard and walked across to the bottom of the stairs. "Is everything OK up there?" she asked, not sure if she wanted to know the answer.
"Yes," confirmed Molly. "But don't come up. It's just Hugh being a pansy," she explained.
"I don't want any hospital trips today!" Ally said, more sternly.
Hugh suddenly appeared at the landing banister.

"Look," he said as he twirled around. "All limbs still attached!"

Ally raised her eyebrows in warning before making her way back to the kitchen. She picked up her cup of tea and walked out of the back door, towards the little stream at the bottom of the garden. She took a seat in her favourite spot and pondered Ben's words.

Meanwhile, Hugh made his way back into Molly's room, to continue helping her string up the fairy lights around the ceiling. "I want it to look like the ceiling is covered in loads of stars," explained Molly.
Hugh handed Molly another set of lights. "I think you'll achieve that," he said sarcastically as he went back to hammering a piece of wood onto the wall, to complete the wooden frame. He climbed down off Molly's bed and rummaged through the bags that were sprawled out across the floor. "Which bag are the stickers in?" he asked as he discarded yet another bag.
"The blue one," Molly confirmed as she hung up the final fairy light. "Now for the big test," she said as she plugged them in and switched them on. Molly shut the curtains and Hugh paused a moment. They both looked up.

The room descended into magic. "Ooh," gasped Molly. "They look amazing!" She jumped

19

up and down, and waved her arms in the air. "Such a good idea," beamed Hugh. He finally found the stickers and stood up. They both whirled around the room as if they were flying through the universe. "Come on," he instructed. "Let's do the last bit." He pounced up onto Molly's bed and wrote inside the frame, using the stickers to form the words. *Molly's Map of Dreams*.

Molly hugged Hugh. "Thank you," she cried with pure gratitude. "I couldn't have done it without you," she added kindly.

"We're the dream team," Hugh confirmed as he hugged her back. "Now, come on, let's do my room before Mom and Ben come back. And then we can do the grand unveiling." Hugh drew the curtains back, and the room was, once again, illuminated with sunlight. He glanced down and saw Ben and Tom walking across from the stables to the house.

"Well, I can't thank you enough," Ben said as he stopped by the side of Tom's truck. He held out his hand.

"Anytime, mate," answered Tom easily. "Just get our names down for some of those rodeos this season," he said as he shook Ben's hand firmly. Ben nodded in agreement. "I'll get that done this week," he confirmed. Tom slid into the driver's side of his truck and started up the engine. Ben took a step back just as Ally appeared from around the side of the house. She joined him and slid her hand around Ben's waist. They both waved as Tom steered his truck down the driveway.

Ben took Ally's hand and they both turned to face the house. "Well, it's still standing," said Ben playfully. "So things can't have gone that wrong." "I think Hugh will have a few bruises in the morning," answered Ally with a wink. They both started to walk towards the front door, their footsteps in time. Ben reached forwards and opened the door to allow Ally to step through first. They were suddenly greeted by Hugh and Molly who were standing there, with large grins on their faces. "We are ready!" they said in unison.

Ally and Ben both looked at each other. "Lead the way," said Ben, gesturing towards the stairs. As they all filed up, Ally and Ben could see that both bedroom doors were closed.
Molly stood outside her door, and slowly reached for the handle. "Welcome to my new bedroom!" she announced proudly as she gave the door a gentle push.
Ally was the first to walk in, quickly followed by Ben. They looked around the room as Molly joined Ben by his side. "Oh, Molly! It's wonderful!" declared Ally as her hands flew to her mouth in

shock.

Ben placed a hand on Molly's shoulder and gave it a squeeze. He took in the new bed sheets, curtains, Molly's Map of Dreams, the fairy lights and the rug on the floor. "I think I'll move in here instead," he declared, clearly impressed. "And, you can have my room."

Molly hugged him tightly. "You're not mad with me for changing things?" she asked in concern.

Ben knelt down and took Molly in his arms. "No," he reassured her. "You have made me the happiest man alive," he added as he kissed her on the forehead.

"OK, my turn!" Hugh said impatiently.

Ally gave Molly a proud smile and then turned to Hugh. "Alright, Monkey. Let's see what you've created." Ally proceeded to follow Hugh back out onto the landing as he shoved his door open with great excitement.

"Tah-dah!" he declared as he stepped inside. Ally followed him and was soon joined by Ben and Molly. They looked at the wall, which had the same wooden frame, but with *Hugh's Map of Dreams* spelled out. Then surveyed his new curtains and bed sheets, his table lamp that shone stars onto the ceiling, and a bean bag in the corner with a bookshelf by the side, stacked with magazines.

"Hugh, I hope you keep it this clean and tidy," said Ally cheekily.

Ben pulled the curtains closed, and lay on the centre of the floor. Hugh flopped down too. "Look," Hugh instructed. "These are all the different stars and formations in the night sky," he explained as he pointed at the ceiling. "Maybe," mused Ben. "One of these nights, we could light the fire-pit, drink hot chocolate out in the garden and see if we can find any of them." "That would be brilliant!" answered Hugh eagerly.

"Come on, Molly," Hugh said suddenly. "Let's go and see Firefly and Red Rock. I missed them so much!" He sprang to his feet, grabbed Molly's hand and pulled her towards the stairs.

Ben continued to look up at the ceiling. For just a moment, every part of him shone with pure joy and pride. Never in a million years would he have thought that his deepest heart's desire would come true. And yet, here he was living it. Ally held out her hand. "Let's get a take-out tonight," she suggested. "And watch a movie." The tiredness of the trip was getting harder to suppress.

Ben slowly got to his feet. "You unpack," he said. "And I'll order the food." He took Ally's hands, placed one on his back and the other in his hand. He began to sway gently, dancing to the rhythm of his heartbeat, under the stars.

Ally rested her head on his chest. "Sounds like a plan," she said as Ben took a step back and twirled her around. Before they stepped out onto the landing, Ben gave Ally's hand an encouraging squeeze.

Ally smiled gleefully as she walked towards their bedroom. Her footsteps were light as a feather as she floated on love. She lifted up her suitcase and placed it on the bed. She whizzed the zip around and flipped it open. She took out her clothes and other items, and placed them back where they belonged. As she put the pieces of her new life back together, she knew that nothing could ever break this picture. As she stepped into the en-suite, she heard the sound of Hugh running up the stairs, soon followed by a "Geronimo!" as he flung his duvet over the banister. It fell to the living room floor, as Ally heard a sweet "and mine too," called up the stairs. Hugh disappeared into Molly's room and did the same with her duvet.

Ally began to hum contentedly as her happiness started to bloom. She somehow knew that everything was going to be alright. She studied her reflection in the mirror. For all the tests, trials and lessons life had brought so far, they had made it, and now was the moment for them to receive the gifts for all their hard work.

The blessings were ready to arrive, like confetti floating in the air. Ally playfully skipped out of the bathroom, zipped up her empty suitcase and put it away.

Ally started to moon walk back along the landing and twirled at the top of the stairs. She punched the air with her hand, in a celebration of liberation. She was snapped back into reality as she heard the front door open. "The food has arrived," shouted Ben. Hugh and Molly rushed into the kitchen and grabbed plates as Ben unpacked and opened the boxes. He also pulled out a bottle of red wine and took two glasses out of the cupboard. Ally entered the kitchen and the smell of food made her stomach rumble with delight. Ben poured a glass of wine and handed it to Ally as Molly ducked under the archway of their arms, and disappeared into the living room with Hugh.

Ben then poured himself a glass and they clinked their glasses together. "Here's to home and family," Ally said as her eyes sparkled with pure bliss.

"I'll raise a glass to that," answered Ben before taking a sip.

"I didn't realise how hungry I was," declared Ally as she began to pile food onto her plate.

"I can tell," laughed Ben as he added food to his,

but slightly more selectively.

"Come on, slow coaches," called Hugh.
"Doesn't that boy ever learn?" asked Ally. "We will never be quick enough for him on movie night!" Ally smiled and shook her head. Ben took hold of his glass and plate, and made his way into the living room. He plonked himself down next to Molly. Ally soon joined them and sat down next to Ben.

"Yay! We can start!" cried Hugh as he pressed the play button on the remote with a sticky finger.
"You'll never guess who I saw today," Ally began. Hugh quickly pressed the pause button and shot a deathly look in his mom's direction. Ally thrust a forkful of food into her mouth as she attempted to supress a mischievous giggle. Hugh once again pressed play as Ally finished her mouthful and continued. "Like I was saying," she said. "It was such a coincidence!"

Hugh angrily pressed pause on the remote again. "MOM!" he yelled. "Seriously," he spat out. A few pieces of chicken followed and fell onto the floor in front of him. This caused them all to erupt into laughter, as tears streamed down Ally's cheeks. Molly clutched her sides and Ben threw back his head. The house filled with the sound of laughter, as Hugh, once again, pressed play and turned up the volume. But he couldn't prevent his giggles escaping like popping bubbles too.

2 LOVE LIGHTING UP THE WAY

"Come on, you two. It's time to go up the apple and pears," yawned Ally as she reached over for the controller and switched off the TV. Molly and Hugh peeled themselves, sleepily, off the sofa and began to make their way towards the staircase. "Night-night," they said in unison before heading up the stairs and into their new bedrooms.

Ally got up and made her way towards the kitchen. But, she looked curiously across at Ben, who was deep in thought, chewing the end of his thumb. "Right," he said enthusiastically, pushing his body to standing. "I am just going to do final checks," he said, marching towards the front door. He grabbed his coat and boots before disappearing outside into the darkness.

Ally finished making her cup of tea. She

peered out of the kitchen window, only just able to make out the outline of Ben's figure, before he disappeared around the side of the trees in front of the barn. Something twisted in her stomach. "Something's not quite right," she said aloud to herself. "Something's changing. What is he up to?" Her questions continued as she made her way up to the bedroom.

Ben walked quietly through the barn, his footsteps in time with the sound of the horses munching on their hay. He peered into each stable to check they had enough water, and were content. When he reached the end of the barn he took hold of the handle of the big barn door and slid it back. Moonlight instantly shone in, and filled the barn with mystery. He leant against the door frame and looked out onto the moonscape. The full moon shone brightly and the sky was speckled with stars. "OK, life," he said. "I need some help here, some inspiration or a clue on what I need to do, even if I don't like it. But, it's not just me anymore. I need to support this family. How do I do it?" he questioned as he sunk his hands deep into his pockets. A shiver ran up his body.

Ben continued to look out onto the land, but everything remained still. The sound of the horses soothed his restless soul. His head flopped forwards as a tear rolled down his cheek. "I am so lost," he sobbed. "I don't know what direction to go in. Please someone, help me," he whispered as his heart cried out. He slowly slid down the barn door frame until he was sitting on the floor, with his knees bent towards his chest. Another tear fell and his body grieved for the loss of the man he was, as he tried to make room for the man he was to become.

Out of the corner of his eye, he saw a horse appear over the stable door. Firefly's head became illuminated by the moonlight. "It might be time for us to hit the road again, Buddy," said Ben sullenly. Firefly suddenly kicked the door with her front hoof and shook her head sideways. "I know," Ben soothed. "I don't want to leave this place either. But I just don't know what else to do?" Firefly disappeared back into the stable and reappeared with a mouthful of hay. She threw it over the stable door and onto the barn alley. "I am not going to start making hay, if that's what you're suggesting," Ben said as he looked at her. Firefly pinned her ears back in protest and continued to stare, intensely, at Ben, waiting for the same idea to reach his mind.

Ben shuffled uncomfortably on the cold floor. He vigorously searched his mind for what Firefly was trying to tell him. A pain began to burn inside of him as he broke eye contact with Firefly and went back to looking out onto the countryside. Firefly stayed motionless as she held her gaze, willing him to remember. Ben felt Firefly's intensity. "What is it that you're trying to tell me, girl?" he asked. "How can hay help me?" Ben got back to his feet and pulled the barn door closed in annoyance. He felt the words on the tip of his tongue, yet he just couldn't quite reach them. As he marched back through the barn, Firefly watched him as he went. "Sorry Firefly, I guess I am just not good enough to figure it out." Firefly lowered her head so that her nose nearly touched the floor as the barn descended into darkness and Ben walked out.

Ben slowly made his way back across to the house. His footsteps felt sticky with frustration as he flung words and ideas around in his mind. They bounced around, ricocheting off his skull. "I am missing something," he muttered. "And I know it's staring me right in the face." He ran up the steps, but as he took hold of the front door handle, he froze. An idea shot through him like a lightning bolt. He suddenly heard his grandpa's voice: *Use your strengths. They open the door to receive great gifts from us all. But you have to act first and put in a little effort into believing it will open. YOU have to push the door open and not just expect it to open by itself.*

Ben quickly let go of the front door handle and bolted back to the barn. As he opened the door and flipped on the light switch, he saw the horse's eyes flicker at the sudden, bright light. He cautiously made his way across to where the hay was stacked. There, hung up, was a finely woven, thin piece of rope on a nail. On the beam was a knife in a leather case. His hand shook as he reached across and lifted the knife off the beam. He slid it out of the leather case. The knife handle was wood and deer antler. His fingers traced the tooling of an intricate pattern on the antler, finely filled with a beautiful basket-woven pattern along the edge. Towards the end, was his name, *Ben*, carved into it.

He lowered himself down and perched on a bale of hay. As he surveyed the knife, he was transported back to the day he had sat on the steps, on the front porch, and made the knife. He had felt a sudden rush of pride and joy when he completed it, knowing that it would outlast him, and someday be passed onto his son, and his son after that. Firefly broke Ben's thoughts as she whinnied in an approving way and stared at him once more. Ben looked up at her and smiled. He continued to recall that day when his grandpa stepped out and perched next to him, when he was just a little boy. *"You have a true gift there, son,"* he had said to him. Ben chuckled. He had

31

felt so much love and passion when he made the knives, but when his grandpa had died, he put them and his tools away, in a box, and shoved it to the very darkest corner of the barn.

Ben took a deep breath and put the knife back in its place. He walked across to the corner of the barn that always remained in the dark. He brushed the cobwebs away with his finger tips and reached forwards. They soon found what he was looking for and he slid a wooden chest out from the dark and into the light. It screeched as it slid across the floor. His fingers flipped the latch open and it creaked an old sigh. Ben slowly opened the lid and peered inside. There, lay the finished and unfinished knives, the leather cases and his tools, all frozen in time, exactly where he had left them the day his grandpa had returned to the stars.

Ben closed the lid and fastened the catches. He took hold of the handles at each end of the chest, stood up and carried it out of the barn. He paused though and placed it down on the floor. He took a carrot from a nearby bucket and walked over to Firefly. She eagerly took it from his hands and munched with great satisfaction. "Thank you," he whispered sweetly, before returning back to the chest and picking it up. He headed out of the barn, flipping the lights off as he went. He felt like he was walking on air as he suddenly realised that his smile was as broad as it was after he had first met Ally.

Ben walked back into the house and headed straight into his office. He placed the chest on the ground, and pulled out a pad of paper and a pen. He sat, purposefully, in his chair and began to scribble furiously on the paper. Ideas and thoughts began to form the building blocks of a plan. His thoughts flourished as if a barrier had been lifted and all that had been lingering behind it, in the back of his mind, could now come to light. He glanced back down at the chest and, there on top, was a single ladybird. Ben paused. He placed his pen down and turned in his chair to look at the ladybird. "I wonder," he muttered as he reached for a book from his shelf. He flicked through the pages until he came across the image of a ladybird. "The symbol of good luck and a wish coming true," Ben read aloud.

He closed the book, placed it back on the shelf and picked his pen back up. He continued to write, periodically looking across at the ladybird, still sitting on the chest. "Well, you know my wish, Ladybird," he said to the silent room. The clock's hands on the office-clock moved past the minutes and the hours as Ben continued to plan. He was eventually brought out of his thoughts when a thin slither of sunlight shone onto his page. He glanced up and looked out of the office window to see the sun beginning to peak over the hillside. The sky was alight with reds and oranges - a vibrant, colourful display, heralding in a new day.

Ben placed his pen down, rubbed his eyes and looked up at the clock. "Jeez," he said wearily. "Is it really that time?" He got up from the desk and stretched his arms up into the air as his body unfroze from its seated position. He slowly opened the office door and made his way across to the kitchen, to make a fresh pot of coffee.

Ally sleepily reached out her hand but found that the bed was empty and cold. But, for the first time, instead of fear flowing through her veins, a pang of curiosity stirred. *Where has he been all night,* she thought. Ally gently got out of bed and grabbed her bath robe from the back of the door. She threaded it on as she walked down the landing. She took in a deep breath and her lungs filled with the smell of coffee. "Where there is the smell of coffee, Ben is never too far away," she chuckled as her hand glided down the banister and she made her way down the stairs.

Ally walked across to the kitchen, her eyes still adjusting to the morning light. As she turned the corner, BANG! Her toe hammered into a solid object. She quickly lifted her foot and squeezed her toe. She closed her eyes tightly shut, trying to block out the pain. "Awww," she moaned through gritted teeth. "Why is it always the same flipping toe?" Ben got up from his seat, wordlessly guided Ally to the nearest chair and passed her a much-needed cup of tea.

Ally opened her eyes and glared down at the offending object. "What the hell is that?" she asked, gesturing towards the chest on the kitchen floor.

Ben joined her at the table. "That is the solution," he explained. "Well, potentially."

Ally took a gulp of tea to soothe the pain as her toe continued to throb. "What are you talking about?" she questioned in confusion.

Ben wrapped his hands around his coffee mug. "I found this on the office desk," he said, sliding a sheet of paper across to her.

Ally glanced down to find that it was the piece of paper she had written earlier, about her dream job. "That was just me messing around," she said casually. "I am going to call up a few of those adverts today instead." She lowered her foot to the floor as the pain began to subside.

Ben scowled at her. "I hope you don't mean that," he responded. "Because there is no reason why you can't have your dream job. Why do you have to do something you don't enjoy just because everyone else is?" he added.

Ben took a swig of coffee. "Because I want to hire you," he said confidently. Ally looked bewildered. "Well, actually," he ventured. "I want us to build this and run this together." Ben continued to wait for the penny to drop, but Ally remained motionless. "Let me explain," said Ben as he reached down to open up the chest. He lifted one of the knives out and its leather case. Ally's eyes widened with delight. "Oh my goodness," she exclaimed. "Where did you get this from? It's beautiful! Look at the craftsmanship! Wow! You don't see this quality anymore. It's wonderful." Ally took it from Ben and rolled it around in her fingers to survey it from every angle.
Ben's cheeks began to redden in embarrassment. "I made it." he said quietly.

Ally looked at him in disbelief. "You have a true gift," she said with genuine admiration. Ben coughed, trying to clear the uncomfortableness that he was feeling. "Thank you," he muttered. "Well, my idea is that you set up an online shop, and we sell them. I'll do the making, and you do the business and running of it." He looked guardedly at Ally, hoping she would say yes. "Then you get to do your dream job, because everything you put down on your list fits perfectly. And we'll make the extra money we need. What do you think?" he asked.

Ally continued to study the knife. "Do you think you'll have enough time?" she asked carefully. "I mean with all the things that need doing on the ranch, and making these?" she added, secretly loving the idea.

"Yes," answered Ben confidently. "I am going to ask Dad to come and help, one day a week, and if Hugh and Molly do their chores too, it will free up some of my time to make them," he explained, still searching Ally's reaction.

Ally held her hand out to Ben. "I think you've got yourself a new business partner," she said as she reached to shake it.

But Ben pushed her hand aside and wrapped his arms around her. He let his lips land on hers.

"This is how we seal our deals," he said tenderly.

Ben lowered himself back into his seat.

"I can't believe you made this," breathed Ally. "It's stunning! How come you're only sharing this now?" she asked, taking his hand.

"Because I had pushed it so far to the back of my mind that I had forgotten all about it," said Ben with shame.

"Well, I don't think we'll be able to keep up with the orders," replied Ally. "People are going to love them! Maybe some of the local shops could sell them for us too?" Ally's mind began to whirl with ideas.

Bang! Ally and Ben suddenly looked up above them, where the noise had come from - Hugh's bedroom.

Hugh sleepily rolled over in his bed. His eyes began to flicker open and his body was still limp in slumber. But, as he turned, he saw the outline of a figure, lying next to him. He gasped as he scrambled and promptly fell out of bed with a thump, onto the floor. "Ouch!" he groaned as he rubbed his bum. He pulled himself up as he peered over the edge of the bed, and saw Molly laying there, looking bewildered. Hugh clambered back into bed. "How long have you been there?" he asked as he pulled his duvet up over his head. "Since before dawn," replied Molly. "I couldn't sleep. I just can't stop thinking about that mirror." Hugh slowly lowered the duvet from above his head. "What about it?" he said, looking at her in confusion.

"I think we should have it outside," answered Molly. "In between our rooms, so we can practice every day," she added as she rolled her thumbs around each other.

"Well, that's easy enough to sort out," said Hugh casually. "Why would you be worrying about that?" he asked, still perplexed by it all.

"I don't know. I just feel something in my gut,"

explained Molly. "It's trying to tell me something, but I just can't understand what it is," she added as she rolled over towards Hugh and huffed.

"OK, anything I can help with?" Hugh asked, feeling a little helpless.
"No, not really," Molly said distantly. "Anyway, we best get up for breakfast. I have already heard Ally and Ben downstairs." Molly climbed over Hugh and whipped back his side of the duvet. "Come on," she ordered cheekily. Hugh shivered as a rush of cold air flew up his body. He scampered out and followed her. They broke out into a run as they bounded down the stairs towards the kitchen, to find Ally and Ben sitting at the table.

"Morning, you two," said Ally, nursing her tea...and toe!
"Morning, Mom," Hugh said, giving her a kiss as he sidled by.
"We need you two to sit at the table for a moment," said Ally. "Family meeting before you start on breakfast," she explained.

Molly and Hugh glanced at each other curiously. "Is everything OK?" Molly asked as she slid into her usual spot at the table.
"Yes, everything is fine," Ally said reassuringly. "We just need to make some changes around here now that there are four of us living in this

house."

Ben carefully placed the knife in the centre of the table. "Wow!" exclaimed Hugh. "Where did you get that from? Can I have one?" he asked in amazement as he carefully reached for it, making sure not to hurt himself.

"Be careful," warned Ben warily. "That is very sharp. I made it a long time ago and yes, you can have one, as long as you learn how to use it properly and safely," Ben stated.

"I will! I promise!" replied Hugh, his eyes wide with excitement.

Molly tilted her head to the side. "I don't get it," she said. "What has that got to do with our family?"

Ben placed his hands out in front of him. "Well, Ally and I are going to start selling them," Ben began. "We are going to create an online shop. But, for this to work, we need your help," he continued. "You know how much time and effort it takes to keep this ranch ticking over, and I am going to need time in my workshop, which means less time on the ranch."

Hugh lifted up his hand, a signal for Ben to stop. "Say no more," he said in allegiance. "We will take over the running of the ranch."

Ben began to laugh. "Just hold your horses a second there. I don't think I am quite ready to hand over the reins completely. But I will need you to pitch in with the care of the horses and Billy will be helping with the maintenance. If we all work together, we should be just fine." Ben smiled.

"So, if we are looking after the horses," said Molly. "Does that mean I can have Red Rock?" she added as she sweetly swayed from side to side, grinning up at Ben.
"We will see," replied Ben, raising his eyebrows.
"This also means that I need your help too," Ally chipped in. "And for your dirty socks and clothes to go in the wash basket, and not next to it," she stated firmly. Hugh let out a groan.
"Maybe we could help cook one night a week as well?" suggested Molly.
"That's a great idea," Ally said.

"Hang on, everyone," said Hugh. "Before you put too many new ideas on the table, let me just go and get..." But, he didn't finish his sentence before he disappeared into the office. He quickly returned with a sheet of paper and some coloured, felt-tip pens. "Right, so if I do the days of the week along there," he mumbled to himself. "And our names down there," he added. "Right, I am ready!" he stated brightly.

"OK, let's start with morning chores," said Ben as he began to reshuffle all the jobs around in his head. "If you two turn out the horses in the barn and do the feeds, I will put a bale of hay out for them in the pasture," he said.

"Slow down," instructed Hugh. "I can't write that quickly."

"While you do that, I can set everything up for breakfast," Ally interjected. "Then after breakfast, I can go into the office," she continued.

"And I can go into the workshop," Ben added.

"Then in the evening, you two muck out the stalls and bring in the horses, and will see to the cattle," Ben said with a smile as each piece slotted together, perfectly.

"And I will get the orders ready to take to the post office the next day," Ally added optimistically.

Hugh's pen squiggled across the page. He took a step back and looked at the sheet. "I think I got it all," he said with a slight frown. "Oh no, what about Billy?"

"We'll put him down for one day a week, for ranch jobs," said Ben, pointing at Wednesday. Ben looked over the plan. "You know what guys? This may just work," he said with surety.

"Of course it will work!" agreed Hugh with much enthusiasm.

"What will work?" said a voice from behind them. They turned to see Billy standing at the entrance to the kitchen.

Hugh bounced up, stood on his chair and held the piece of paper up. "Well, Ben is going to start making and selling these knives, and we are all going to help around the ranch so that he has some time to do it," he announced excitedly. Billy shot a look across to Ben as he walked over to the coffee pot and poured himself a cup. "I thought you were never going to touch that again?" he mumbled.
Ben scraped his chair back. "Why don't you say that a bit louder?" he responded in anger.

Billy turned around, his sullen eyes peering over the top of his coffee mug. He took a sip and raised his eyebrows in response. Ben turned on his heels and marched out the door. Billy placed his cup down and followed him outside. Ally, Hugh and Molly rearranged themselves around the kitchen table so they could watch out of the kitchen window. "What was that about?" asked Molly as she watched the tension grow rapidly between Ben and Billy.
"I'm not too sure," Ally replied. "But I feel there are more secrets in this box than we have been told about," she stated as she closely studied Ben's expressions.

"Quick! Back into position," Hugh instructed as they watched Billy make his way back into the house and Ben striding out towards the barn.

Hugh and Molly pretended to get things ready for breakfast and Ally sat looking over the new routine. They all listened to Billy grumbling to himself as he walked up the steps and into the house. Molly greeted him by holding out his coffee mug.

"What was all that about?" Molly asked directly.

Billy snapped out of his thoughts and stared at Molly. "Oh, nothing," he replied, taking a seat at the table.

Molly quickly pulled out the chair next to him. "It didn't look like nothing," she said. Billy's eyes narrowed as he scowled at Molly. "You grownups think that you can hide things from us," she said bravely. "But we see it all. We just don't normally bother asking you because we know you're going to lie and just say everything is fine. When we know, full well, it isn't." Molly folded her arms. "Nana O always told me the truth, even though I didn't always want to hear it. But at least I knew where I was with everything," she added as her gaze interrogated Billy for the truth.

Billy rolled his coffee cup around in the palm of his hands as he gathered his thoughts. "It hit Ben hard when his grandpa died. They were very close," he explained. "He used to tell him everything and then Ben suddenly felt like he had no one to talk to. He was...no, he is very talented at his craftsmanship, but when he was younger, he found it very difficult to receive," Billy continued. Hugh stopped what he was doing then and came and sat down at the kitchen table too.

"We are always compensated for everything we do," Billy explained. "That's one of life's laws: the law of compensation."
"I don't understand," said Hugh, puzzled by Billy's explanation.
Billy leant back in his seat as he formulated his words. "For the effort we put in, the tests and trials we make it through, the changes and the skills we learn, we always end up receiving something - a gift, or some say, a blessing. But here's the sticky part. Normally, because the journey hasn't been as easy as people would have liked it to be, their hands are clenched tight with anger and resentment, and they keep looking back and retelling the past. So, when life says, *here is your reward*, they can't receive it until they let go and allow their hands to, shall we say, open, to let life give it to them."

"But I don't understand how that affects Ben?" Molly queried as she shuffled to get comfy on the wooden chair.
Billy let out a sigh. "Ben was so angry and full of resentment at life, for taking away his best friend.

It took him many years to stop walking around with his fists clenched. And in that time, that box down there with all the memories it held, got put in the darkest corner of the barn, never to be seen. Always there but not forgotten. Until you guys came along. You must have sparked something within him which helped him to learn and remember that he is worth something, and to let go of his anger and resentment. Hopefully he will now allow himself to receive the decades of gifts that are stacked up, just waiting to come into his life," Billy said, shaking his head. "Not that I could tell him that, of course. That man has got the will of an ox at times."

"Is this the next lesson for us?" asked Hugh as he wiggled in his chair.
Billy gave him a momentary smile. "Maybe it's your turn to teach Ben," he pondered.
Ally felt a protective passion begin to grow up from her stomach. "Right gang, we know what to do. If we set up the environment for Ben to thrive, then it's up to him to use that opportunity to act," she said as she got up from the table. "If you need me, I will be in the office, building a website." She then looked at each of them, in the eyes. "Don't you lot think you should be doing your chores too?" she asked sternly.
"Aye-aye, Captain!" replied Hugh, before he and Molly ran upstairs to get dressed.

Billy lifted up the piece of paper and glanced over it. "So, I am here Wednesdays doing ranch jobs?" he inquired, looking up at Ally. "I think I'll come every day. There is more to be done on this place than can be achieved in one day of work a week," he said as he placed the paper firmly back on the table.

"Just do what you can," Ally said over her shoulder as she disappeared into the office, in her dressing gown.

As Billy got up from the table, he heard the thunder of little feet patter down the stairs. Hugh and Molly skidded into the kitchen. "First ranch job for you," Hugh said. But Billy stayed quiet and just waited for Hugh to continue. "Please could you hang the mirror outside my and Molly's bedrooms, for us to practice each morning?" Molly swayed sweetly from side to side in the background.

Billy's shoulders noticeably relaxed. "I'll go and get my tool kit and meet you upstairs," he said.

"Yay!" Hugh and Molly cheered as they disappeared back up the stairs.

Billy walked away, shaking his head. "Just like her Nana. Always did have a way to make her wishes come true."

Molly and Hugh waited patiently outside their rooms as they listened to the sound of the front door closing and then Billy's footsteps on the stairs. He appeared with an old tool bag in one hand. "Right then," he said. "Where would you like it?" He placed his bag down on the landing. "Just here," replied Hugh, pointing at the pillar of wall between the two door frames.

"Right you are," stated Billy. He took out his hammer and a nail, and gently tapped it into the wall. "Could you hold this for me?" he asked as he passed the hammer to Molly and reached down to take hold of the mirror. Hugh and Molly had no time to waste and had already carried it out.

Billy carefully hung it on the nail and they all took a step back. He moved the right corner, just slightly, to make sure it was perfectly level. "There," he declared. "That should do it."

Molly and Hugh stood in front of it and stared into their reflections. Then suddenly burst with joy and flung themselves onto Billy with gratitude, nearly knocking him over. "Thank you, thank you, thank you," they repeated like a ticking motor.

"OK, OK. That'll do," said Billy, feeling out of his comfort zone. He patted them on their heads awkwardly. "Right, come on. Let's go and get these jobs done," he said, picking up his tool bag. And they all made their way down the stairs.

As Hugh, Molly and Billy made their way

towards the front door, they nearly crashed into Ally as she was making a beeline for the office, with a fresh cup of tea in hand. "Mom?" Hugh asked, his words drifting.

"Not now, Hugh. I'm busy," Ally answered over her shoulder. But then stopped at her automatic response and turned to face Hugh. "Sorry, Monkey, yes?" she said with more softness.

"I love you," Hugh said, smiling gleefully.

Ally's heart melted and she smiled back. "I love you too, Monkey," she replied, before turning and making her way back into the office - her footsteps just a little lighter.

Billy glanced down at Hugh. "You know her well," he acknowledged with a glint in his eye. Hugh shrugged his shoulders. "Someone has to keep an eye on her," he said as he slipped on his boots and jacket.

"And someone has to keep an eye on you," said Molly as she gently barged him with her shoulder.

The three of them stepped outside and took a deep breath in. The sweet, fresh air filled their lungs. "Come on, let's get started," said Molly, breaking out into a run. Billy watched Ben coming out of the barn on his tractor, with a large bale. "Right then, I best make a start too," he muttered to himself as he strode out with his tool bag. He walked towards the barn to repair a door –

second job on the list. Ben carefully lowered the bale into the feeder as the horses eagerly shuffled around, trying to sneak a mouthful of hay. Ben hopped out and cut the baling twine. "Come on, you guys! Away with you," he instructed. "At least wait until I'm done," he added, waving his arms towards the horses to create space for him to reach the bale. As each piece of sting pinged and the hay waterfalled into the feeder, the horses made their move. Ben squeezed between them. "Don't mind me then, guys," he said, patting one on the neck as he passed.

Ben climbed back into the tractor and slowly manoeuvred it out of the field and back to the barn. He expertly parked it up, ready for tomorrow. He paused as he watched Molly and Hugh walking up the aisle of the barn, with Firefly and Red Rock, skipping as they went. Ben felt a wave of relief. *Maybe it isn't such a bad thing to ask for help occasionally*, he thought wisely as he climbed down off the tractor. He made his way back to the house to get a fresh cup of coffee, to take into his workshop.

"You know, Son. I may not always say it, or I may never say it, but I am proud of you. Through every challenge, every setback, you have always kept your smile and your faith. You definitely get that from your mother," said Billy. "There could be a hurricane outside and she'd find a way to make it exciting and fun." Billy huffed to himself as he got up and placed a hand on Ben's shoulder. Billy glanced down at the floor as he puffed out his chest. "You've done good, Son, real good," he added as his gaze lifted and met Ben's.

Ben smiled sheepishly. "Umm, thanks, Pa," he said. "I'd best be getting started on those knives before Ally works her sales magic too well." Ben smiled and gave his dad a nod of acknowledgement.

As Ben walked across towards the house, he sunk his hands into his pockets and let a smile creep across his face. He replayed the words his dad had just said - words he had longed to hear for so many years. He didn't need to hear them now, yet here they were. Ben skipped up the steps, through the front door and he made his way to the kitchen. He poured another cup of coffee and placed it on the kitchen table. He listened to Ally, muttering to herself in the office, and took a step towards the office door. He paused. *Actually, on second thoughts, I'd best leave her to it*, he thought as he turned on his heels and went upstairs to get another jumper.

Ben felt a zing of happiness run through his

body as he ran up the stairs. He was excited to reopen the workshop, set out his tools again and turn on the bench lamp. He suddenly screeched to a stop as he reached the top of the stairs though. Sunlight reflected onto the mirror, now hanging there. "Well, well. You have found your place again," said Ben as he slowly walked across towards the mirror.

He paused in front of it as he recalled the first time Molly and Hugh had seen the mirror, and he recited the song, "Mirror, mirror, on the wall. No longer shall you reflect the person I once was, as now I stand tall, seeing, for the first time, a truth like never before. As the veil is lifted between the worlds and I see, there in the reflection, the person I was and am in the dream world. As the light inside my heart begins to shine, illuminating every part of my life, as now I find the person in my dreams is standing there, staring back at me," he whispered. Ben walked across to the bedroom and pulled out his favourite jumper from the drawer. He slipped it on, ran down the landing and the stairs, scooped up his coffee as he passed the kitchen table, and headed out the front door. He felt a new sense of freedom like never before.

3 STORM WARNING

Ben made his way across to the barn and as
he walked past the entrance, he peered inside.
He saw that Billy was still knelt down, fixing the
door. Ben took a sip of coffee as he continued on
his path. He felt the same rush that Ally had
spoken about when she drinks tea. He could feel
the warmth soothe his restless mind. He
eventually reached a hedgerow. The leaves were
ablaze with reds and greens. As he slipped
behind, there stood a small, log cabin. He paused
a moment as the shed wasn't quite like he
remembered. The wood was silvery as it had aged
and weathered the different seasons. And there,
scribed on the door, were the words *Ben's
Workshop*, in a childlike scribble. Ben slowly
blinked as he remembered the day his grandpa
had shown him the cabin as if it was only

yesterday. It was a feeling of pure excitement. His grandpa had built it especially for him. He recalled, now, how he had taken out his new tool and scribed those words into the door.

Ben took in a deep breath as he reached into his pocket and took out an old-fashioned key. He slowly slid it into the lock and listened to the click. The door creaked stiffly open and Ben investigated the darkness. He reached his fingers around the inside of the door frame and flipped a switch. It bathed the cabin in light. The cobwebs glistened in the light and a layer of dust covered whatever lay beneath. Ben took another sip of coffee and waited for the tidal wave of fear, sadness or anger to rush over his body. Yet nothing arrived.

He stepped inside and the floor boards creaked as the log cabin began to wake from its long hibernation. Ben's eyes scanned the room. Everything seemed poised and ready for its master's instructions. Ben placed his coffee cup down on the bench, and reached across to take hold of a broom from the corner. He began to sweep, rhythmically, and with every stroke, a truth began to emerge.

The dust started to rise and fill the air with sparkling particles. Ben continued, little by little, to brush the past out of the door and into mother nature's care. He placed the broom outside the door and then stepped into a place that was so familiar yet almost forgotten. He reached forwards and turned the workbench lamp on. He pulled out a stool and perched on it, simply looking at the emptiness in front of him.

Ben stayed motionless, awaiting his next move. His brow furrowed and his eyes became fixed as he reached forwards and slid out the drawer of a tin box. There inside, lay a row of handles. "It's time," he said to the silent cabin. He picked up one of the handles and rolled it around in his palm. He felt the wood and antler brush against his skin. Ben shuffled to get himself more comfortable as he took a piece of sand paper from a pile on the shelf above him. He blew off the dust before beginning to work, just like he had done once before, but now it was for a reason worth so much more.

As the sun rose higher in the sky, Molly and Hugh bounded around the ranch like two gazelles full of life. But, Hugh suddenly stopped and clutched his stomach as it gurgled and rumbled. Molly paused as she turned and looked at Hugh. "Was that you?" she asked curiously.
"No, of course not," answered Hugh dismissively as his stomach rumbled again. He blushed and Molly erupted into laughter.

"Come on," she said. "Let's go and see what's for lunch before your stomach growls anymore." She bounced up the steps, through the front door and across to the kitchen, with Hugh in hot pursuit.

The house was peacefully silent. "Mom?" called Hugh.
But Molly quickly placed her hand over Hugh's mouth. "Sshh," she instructed. "Don't disturb them."
Hugh fell to his knees. "I can't go any further," he said dramatically as he placed his hand to his forehead.
"You are such a drama queen," Molly said, tutting, as she proceeded towards the bread. "Look, we can make our own lunch. You get the ham, lettuce and tomatoes, and I'll butter some bread," she suggested. Hugh got to his knees and headed to the fridge. He filled his arms with as much food as possible, and his mouth with cucumber, before walking back across to Molly.

Molly lay out all the ingredients and started to make the sandwiches. "Can you go and call everyone?" Molly said over her shoulder.
Hugh glanced around at the deserted ranch. "Umm, I think so," he said, a little baffled as to where everyone had gone. He walked back out of the front door and scanned the landscape. "Where is Patches when you need him, to round

everyone up?" he muttered. As he searched, he saw, out the corner of his eye, an old, iron bell hanging from the corner of the front porch. It had a string hanging down from its centre. "Billy must have fixed that today," said Hugh as he marched towards it.

Hugh took in a large breath of air, filled his lungs and wrapped his fingers around the string. '*Ding a ling a ling*' chimed the bell. Its echo could be heard through the valley. "Food!!!!" yelled Hugh at the top of his lungs.
"Where's the fire?" asked Ally as dashed out of the office, eyes wide with fear.
"No fire," replied Molly. "Just your fog-horn son," she added as she placed the last sandwich on the table. "Lunch is ready."
Ally stretched and stood up straight. "Wow! Is it that time already? I must have lost track. Thank you, Molly," she said gratefully as she sat down at the kitchen table.

Hugh's voice finally tapered off as he reached the end of his announcement. "Are you inviting our neighbours too?" chuckled Billy. "I think they heard you as well," he added as he skipped up the steps and into the house.
Hugh continued to look for Ben as he got ready to refill his lungs again. "Wait, wait, I'm here," called Ben. "No need to do that again," he said as he

57

appeared through the trees with his hands up in the air.

"That's a shame," replied Hugh as he sighed out the excess air in his lungs.

Ben and Hugh stepped inside and sat down at the table. The only sound that could be heard was teeth crunching on fresh lettuce leaves. "So, how's it going?" asked Ally before taking another bite.

Ben could only nod as his cheeks bulged with food. '*Good*' he motioned with a thumbs up. Ally looked across to Billy, who was in the same state, and he, too, gave a thumbs up. "I have no idea where Ben gets his table manners from," Ally said cheekily as she glanced between them both.

"Are we expecting someone?" Hugh queried as he watched a cloud of dust rolling down the driveway. Ally and Ben glanced at each other and shook their heads in confusion. Ben wiped his hands down his jeans as he stood up to get a better look out of the window. "It's a taxi," he informed everyone at the table. Ally raised her eyebrows, still baffled.

"I will laugh so much if it's Grandma," giggled Hugh.

Ally froze in fear. "No, it can't be!" she said. "She would have told us." Ally leapt up to join Ben at the window and squinted to try and see who was in the car.

Molly began to giggle too. "That would be so funny! Can you imagine her here in the countryside?" Billy glanced at the two of them, motioning for them to explain more.
"Oh no! No, no, no! Not today! Not any day!" Ally stuttered as a silhouette stepped out of the car. Ben straightened his back and sunk his hands into his pockets as he let out a deep sigh of disappointment.

They all watched the front door swing open. A woman barked out orders at a taxi driver, who was huffing and puffing as he placed a suitcase on the floor. He stood and tilted his hat at the circle of faces in front of him, all frozen with surprise. They felt a storm approaching and the atmosphere became electric as the figure stepped through the door. Ally gasped.
"It's like you have all just seen a ghost!" the figure screeched.
"Hi, Grandma," Hugh said, breaking the silence. He walked across and hugged her.
"You smell," Ally's Mum stated rudely. "Have you not been showering properly?" she asked as she rubbed her nose.
"It's good to see you too," Hugh replied as he walked back to Molly, took her hand and lead her towards the front door.

"But I haven't finished my sandwich," wailed Molly, trying to resist Hugh's tugging.

"Trust me on this one," Hugh whispered before they slipped outside.

"Right, Ben. We best take a look at that job you wanted me to do," Billy said, signalling frantically with his eyes towards the front door. Ben frowned in confusion as Billy jerked his head towards the door as well.

"Oh, yes. Right, yes that job," Ben stuttered as they both stepped quickly across the hallway.

"Mam," Billy said, tipping his hat as he passed Ally's mum, whilst pushing Ben to go faster with his other hand.

Ally stood like a statue as she watched her mum's laser eyes scan every inch of the house. Ally could tell she was making a mental catalogue of things to complain about. "Well, don't just stand there, Ally," snapped her mum. "You should offer your guest a drink after their long trip. You might as well have moved to the other side of the world, the amount of time it took me to get here," she complained as she placed her coat on the hook.

"I wish," muttered Ally as she turned the kettle on. "What are you doing here anyway? Did I miss an e-mail you sent?" asked Ally, trying to filter through the images in her mind to see where she might have missed something.

Ally's mum screeched out a kitchen chair and purposely sat in Ben's seat. Ally winced protectively at the action. "I am here to help with the preparations," explained Ally' mum. Ally's face continued to look confused. "The wedding, of course," her mum stated firmly.
"But we, erm, haven't...err," Ally stuttered, once again scampering through her thoughts of when they had set a date for, but before she had time to decide again, there was no recollection.
"I sent out the invitations to all the family and closest friends," Ally's mum said casually.

Ally's face froze with shock.
"You...did...what?" she asked, slowly pronouncing each word.
"Look, if I didn't organise things, then nothing would ever happen," replied Ally's mum, smugly. The kettle clicked and Ally gratefully turned her back. She reached for the tea pot and a cup, poured the water inside and added a tea bag, stalling for time, whilst she tried to calm herself down.
"So, this is the place?" Ally's mum said with a hint of disgust. "Terribly dirty," she remarked as she dusted some breadcrumbs off the table.

Ally placed the tea pot down in front of her mum, with a cup and some milk. "I'll be back in a second," Ally said as she strode purposefully towards the front door. She closed it firmly behind her and ran, as fast as she could, towards the barn. She came to an abrupt halt when she found the four of them sitting on the hay bales. "It's alright for you guys to head into the storm bunker whilst I deal with the hurricane in there," she stated angrily. They all remained silent as Ally vigorously shook her head. "She has only gone and sent out invitations to who knows how many people!" she shrieked.

Ben stood up and took a protective step towards her. "What are you talking about, Ally?" he asked. Ally gasped for air. "She has sent out invitations to our wedding, and chosen the date, and who knows what else!" Ben's expression hardened and, for the first time, Hugh knew that Ally's mum had overstepped the mark.

"She can't do that," cried Molly in disbelief. "There is no '*can't*' in my mum's dictionary," Ally explained. "Only herself and her reputation," she added, running her hands through her hair in frustration.

They all continued to sit in silence as the news slowly filtered through. But Ally paced up and down, feeling more and more frustrated with each step. Ben was the first to speak. "When?" was all he asked.

"How am I supposed to know!" Ally angrily shot back.

Hugh slid down from the bale of hay. "I'll go and find out the details," he said. "Everyone wait here." Hugh was not only hurt by his grandma's actions for the first time, but disappointed in her as well. She was supposed to be the adult. Ally's mum listened to some footsteps on the dirt and then as they echoed on the wooden steps. She sneakily smirked her happiness at the reaction she had received from her actions. As she pricked up her ears and smoothed out her clothes, she listened to sound of the front door opening.

But her expression changed. "Oh, Hugh," she said with surprise and undisguised disappointment at not being able to have another argument with Ally.

"Grandma," Hugh began. "Mum's just said that you sent out the invitations to *her* and Ben's wedding?" he said, emphasising the word '*her*' as he spoke. "When did you tell everyone it was?" he asked.

Ally's mum shuffled in her chair and then sat up tall to continue her announcement. "Next Saturday," she replied haughtily.

Hugh breathed as he tried to contain the dragon beginning to rage inside. "Grandma, when did you send out these invitations?" he questioned with

his eyes fixed on his grandma's face.
"I did it as soon as she returned from sorting out
Molly's things," she said casually.
Hugh's eyes widened with disbelief. He took
another deep breath in. "Did you not think to ask
Mum when *she* wanted it?" he said, now through
gritted teeth.

"Hugh, look at these clothes," remarked his
grandma, trying to change the subject.
"Standards are slipping," she said as she scowled
at the dirt on his t-shirt. Hugh watched his
grandma take a sip of tea and the corners of her
mouth curl with gladness. He realised that
everything was going just as she wanted it to. His
heart panged in pain, and he began to see the
side of her that his mum had spoken about, but
that he had always dismissed with claims that
she was making it up. He walked out of the house
and back towards the barn. As he got closer, he
could hear Ally talking rapidly, her words tinged
with fear and anger.

Hugh entered the barn and sat down next to
Molly. Ally paused, awaiting her fate. "Next
Saturday," Hugh whispered. Molly saw his
expression of sadness so took hold of his hand
and gave it a squeeze.
Ally's eyes widened with fear. "Well, she will just
have to ring everyone and tell them it's not

happening, ever!" she cried. "And then she can get on a plane and head back to her dark hole, to conjure up another scheme," she added bitterly. Billy watched a tear form in the corner of Ben's eye. "Just take a seat, Ally," he soothed. "Let's think this through with level heads." Ally opened her mouth, ready to fire words back at Billy, but she felt a small hand take hold of hers. It was Hugh, gently guiding her to the hay bales.
" I don't understand why Grandma is doing this to you," muttered Hugh sadly. "It's like she wants you to be unhappy," he observed as tears rolled down his cheeks.

Ally softened as she reached out to cradle Hugh. "I don't know why she does this, Monkey," Ally replied. "But she always has. It's like she is set to sabotage anything good that happens to me." Ally rocked Hugh from side to side, as much for herself as for him.

"Well, we won't let that happen," Ben said as he turned and stared at Ally, his eyes ablaze with determination. "We are a family," he said as he glanced at each one of them. "With our roots running deep, and our family tree so strong, we can withstand any storm, including your mother. If she wants to play games, that's fine. But she won't be able to win against our dream team," he added with unshakable certainty.

Ally smiled feebly. "You don't know what she's

like," she sighed.

Ben looked at her. "I have met plenty of her kind before," he said. "The kind who would prefer to eliminate all those around them just to survive, instead of work together and thrive."

Ally rubbed her hands over her face. "But we are just starting to organise the new business," she said wearily.

Ben sat down beside her and wrapped his arm around her shoulder. "I know," he said sadly. "But, we don't have to give up on that dream either. We just need some help."

A sudden thought bolted through Molly's mind. "We need Sally," she cried.

"We need Jane," added Ally.

"We need an army," Billy finished.

"Well, then that's what we will do," Ally said. "We will build this dream together, as a family." She let her head flop back. "But there is so much to organise. And we may not be able to find a venue at such short notice."

"You could have it here," Molly suggested.

"We can fix the place up a bit," Billy added.

"Where there is a will, there is always a way, Miss Ally," Ben said, kissing her on the lips.

"Right! Let's make a plan," shouted Hugh, clapping his hands together.

"Well first of all, we need to get the Wicked Witch of the West out of the house for a few hours," stated Ally.

"Me and Hugh can do that," Molly said, now smiling.

"Then we need to go into the office and call everyone we know who could possibly help us organise this in a week," said Ally. As the words left her lips, she had a sudden realisation of the size of the task ahead.

"Done," said Billy reassuringly. "And, I will keep going at that job list, which I'm sure is going to triple in size in the next 24 hours. I think it's time Molly and Hugh learnt how to safely use a hammer," he added with a wink.

"Firstly," stated Ben as he looked at Ally. "You need to march into that kitchen with your head held high, casually tell your mum that it's no problem at all, and show her that this family doesn't crumble under pressure. Instead, it creates something beautiful," he added with a proud smile.

Ally gingerly stood up and looked at the pillars of strength that were her family members. They were all standing tall and supporting their dreams. Yet she felt that she was going to crack and crumble, and be the one who allowed the dream to fall and shatter. She took a slow, deep breath in, frantically seeking strength. She slowly began to put one foot in front of the other, and felt the gaze of everyone, pushing her forwards like an invisible force.

Ally stepped out of the barn and into the sunshine. She momentarily closed her eyes and felt the sun warm her skin. When she opened them again she focused, like a laser beam, on the front door. "This has to end, once and for all," she declared. "It's time for me to be set free." With that, she stomped towards the house, with her arms swinging determinedly.

Ally's mum was peering out of the window and she watched Ally heading her way. She scampered back to her seat, picked up her empty cup and pretended to sip the last few drops. She eagerly awaited the forthcoming argument. Ally paused as she wrapped her fingers tightly around the door handle, causing her knuckles to go white. "Calm and casual," Ally whispered to herself.

Ally stepped into the house and headed softly towards the kettle to make herself a cup of tea. "Would you like a fresh one?" Ally asked, waving her empty cup towards her mum.
"Yes," Ally's mum replied. Her piercing gaze was directed towards Ally. She was waiting for the flag to be lifted and for the argument to begin. Ally recognised that look so well. She had been so afraid of it, but now instead, all she felt was pity

that her mum got such a thrill from this. Ally continued to make two cups of tea, and as she walked across to the fridge to fetch the milk, she couldn't help but smile at her own small victory.

" Oh, by the way," Ally said casually. "I have just spoken with Ben." She could see her mum shuffle to the edge of her seat, out of the corner of her eye.

"Yes," replied her mum.

Ally passed her a cup of tea. "And we are in agreement that the wedding should be held next Saturday." Ally watched as the cup slid straight through her mum's hands and crashed to the table, causing a tidal wave of tea to cascade over her lap. Her mum sat, mimicking a fish, as her mouth opened and closed, but no words came out.

Ally raised her eyebrows and gave a sweet smile. "The towels are under the sink," she said as she continued to walk back towards the door. Ally's mum's eyes moved rapidly from side to side. She was desperately seeking the thread to pull that would tear Ally's dreams apart. Yet, she found nothing. Ally reached for the door. Her hand was shaking but she quickly stepped outside and walked briskly back to the barn. She saw four heads peeking out and she signed a thumbs up with her hand. She then watched four smiles beam a light of hope in her direction.

"OK then," said Hugh, clapping his hands together. "Me and Molly will go and occupy Grandma for a couple of hours, while you go into your office and rally the troops."
"Ben and I will create a list of the repairs that need to occur around the ranch," offered Billy. "And can you give Tom a call to see if they can come down for a few days to help out?" he added. Ally perched on a hay bale. She suddenly felt overwhelmed and cold as her mind whirled.

Hugh and Molly were the first to exit the barn. They casually made their way back to the house as they cooked up a plan to keep Hugh's grandma as far away from the ranch as possible. Billy was the next to leave and he made his way to get the truck, with his notepad and pen. Ben glanced across to Ally, only to see her face turn a new shade of white. "Ally," he said tenderly as he crouched down in front of her. "You have fought so long on your own, and been so strong for you and Hugh. But now it is time to let the family work together, to make this dream come true," he said as he gently ran his hand down the side of her cheek.

Ally's eyes briefly closed. "Why is it so hard to receive your own dreams?" she whispered.
"Because," replied Ben. "To receive, means to

accept the change. And most of the time, we just prefer to think about the change and not actually do the changing. It's far easier that way. But easy isn't always right," he explained to her.

Ally sighed. "I have wanted this moment for so long. But I know that I have grown so used to thinking about it and wanting it, that having it now seems so outrageous," Ally said as her forehead wrinkled in confusion.

"You know nature's laws," Ben replied. "You are the key to opening the door of opportunity in front of you," he said, his eyes fixed on Ally's.

Ally paused and thought. "But how can I receive what I want when there are so many other people involved who all want something different?" she queried as she continued to push the responsibility away.

"Each person can want different things," Ben said wisely. "But no one has to go without. Nature doesn't do 'either/or', she only does 'and', which means that the dream of each individual is an extension of your dream. Like the branches on a tree, all growing in their own direction, but still anchored together."

Ally huffed. She knew Ben was right. "I best start making some phone calls then," she said as she stood and her body got its feeling back.

Ben interlocked his fingers with hers as they

walked out of the barn together. "Go and get yourself something that brings you hope," he said to her. "Something that makes you smile, and believe that this is the symbol of receiving one of your deepest desires."

"I will," replied Ally as she gently squeezed his hand.

They made their way out of the barn and across the yard. Ben kissed Ally on the forehead just as they heard the front door opening. Ally's mum stepped out and Ally's gaze drifted down to the large tea stain on her mum's clothes. Hugh and Molly appeared out from behind her. "We are just going to show Grandma around the ranch," Hugh shouted. Ben felt Ally's body stiffen at the sight of her mum, so gave her a gentle push on her lower back to stop her feet from freezing. Ally played her part and painted on a smile as she walked past and into the house.

"No problem, Hugh," confirmed Ben. "Just make sure you close the gates behind you," he added as he climbed into Billy's truck. Billy already had the engine running, ready for a quick escape. He immediately pulled off and they made their way down to the lower pastures. Billy glanced across at Ben and raised his eyebrows. Ben flopped his head back against the head rest, suddenly exhausted at the thought of what was to come, but he couldn't show Ally for he knew he needed to be her rock right now. "I know son," said Billy. "Families are complicated things. You can't do right for wrong sometimes," he added, trying to lighten the mood. Ally headed towards the house as she watched Hugh, Molly and her mum walk through the gate and begin to climb the hill. "Come on, Grandma! We want to show you the best place ever!" she heard Hugh call.

Ally smiled. One thing was for sure. Her mum would be going to bed early tonight after one of Hugh's adventures. She stepped into the house but a shiver ran down her spine and her body quivered. The house felt darker than usual and the air felt heavier. She walked briskly over to the large windows and opened the patio doors, wide. The sound of the stream at the bottom of the garden drifted through the room as she headed into the office. She plonked herself down in the chair and her hand hovered over the telephone, ready to call her first knight in shining armour: Jane.

Ring, ring, ring, ring. Ally's eyes opened wide as she slowly picked up the phone. She placed it to her ear and muttered a shaky, "hello."
"Ally, is that you?" said a familiar voice down the line.
"Jane?" replied Ally.

73

"Yes, yes it is. Oh my goodness, it arrived in the post this morning. I bet you didn't have anything to do with this!" Jane said firmly down the phone. Ally could hear the same frustration in Jane's voice that she felt inside.

"I was just about to call you," Ally said, now feeling confused at the weird coincidence.

"No need," replied Jane. "Are you going through with it?" Jane paused. The silence was deafening. Ally was nodding her head. "Ally, you're going to have to speak to me. I can't see you," Jane instructed impatiently.

"Oh, right," stuttered Ally. "Sorry. Yes, we have decided to go through with it."

Jane fell silent. "That control toad," she eventually managed. Jane took in a gasp of air. "Well, she will get what she gives out, that's for sure," Jane ranted.

"I don't want any trouble," Ally replied softly. "I am tired of these battles with her. If she wants to play these games, then she can go ahead. But I'm just not going to let them get to me anymore."

Jane remained silent for a moment as she thought carefully about her next few words. "Ally, you're a good woman, with a pure heart. I know you have made some mistakes in the past, we all have. But, trust me when I say, all the good you have given to others, even if it was just a thought, will be returned to you in such magical ways," she said kindly.

"I do hope so," sighed Ally. "I am really ready for things to start going our way." A tear escaped down her cheek.

"Ally, you and your family have experienced loss and change on such a gigantic level," soothed Jane. "Yet, even when you were at your lowest and the pain was at its highest, you still met us all and the day ahead, with love and kindness. Compensation for all that you have done won't just be coming to you in money, even though we both know that Molly, especially, has been compensated very well. But, just watch as you become surrounded by people who love you, people who will help you for a change, to make one of your dreams come true. I know, let's play a game. For every effort of sabotage on your mum's part, let's find out how it is compensated with a blessing, to restore the balance?" Jane suggested, sounding so sure.

"Well, Jane," replied Ally. "You have been right about a lot of things. And I won't be surprised if you are right about this. Game on!" Ally said as she felt her strength begin to return.

"Right, that's settled then. I am booking my flight. I will be with you as soon as I can, and I will bring reinforcements," Jane stated. "And plenty of tea!" Ally let her head hang. "First blessing received. Thank you," she whispered.

"Ally, after all those times you have been there for us, now it's time to receive the compensations for those actions. And you deserve to have the best day ever," Jane said, her voice softer now.

"Let me know when your plane arrives," Ally said. "And I will come and pick you up. And, we will sort out a place for you to stay."

"Perfect, see you soon," Jane said as she hung up the phone.

Ally paused, and her hand hovered over the phone again. She watched it curiously, but this time it remained silent. She picked up a piece of card from the desk and typed the number from it into the phone. She waited, listening to the ring tone. "Hello," a breathless voice eventually said. "Tom. It's Ally," she said into the receiver.

"Oh, hi, Ally," greeted Tom. "Just give me a second while I tag this calf." Ally listened to the phone being set down and then the ensuing scuffle. "Right, all yours," Tom said as he came back on the line. Ally paused. What was she meant to say? "Is everything ok?" Tom asked, hearing her hesitation.

"Yes and no," replied Ally. "We are all fine, but Ben and I need your help. It's a long story, but we are going to have the wedding soon. Is there any chance you could come to the ranch for a few days? You'll probably need to bring your trailer for a place to sleep." Ally held her breath.

"Say no more," replied Tom easily. "I will head down the day after tomorrow, and pick up Chad on the way," he added determinedly.

"Thank you," Ally sighed, feeling a huge wave of relief.

Ally continued to make phone calls, connecting with all those she had met along the journey so far. She felt the warmth of support wrap around her as she heard the familiar voices of Billy and Helen, the excitement from Adan in the background, and as Sally shouted out the news to John. One by one, she felt this army of people link together. People who have shown love and kindness to her and her family, and who would now create a bubble around her and Ben's dream.

Hugh continued to climb, with Molly hot on his heels. They both strode out, yearning to reach their favourite place, feeling more and more inspired with each footstep. They were serenaded from behind by the exhausted breathing sounds of Ally's mum. "Hugh, stop!" ordered his grandma. "Just stop! I need to take a break. I am old you know."

"Oh, come on," urged Hugh. "We're nearly there," As he turned around, he could see the beads of sweat on his grandma's forehead. Ally's mum firmly stopped her feet in protest. She turned and sat down on the ground without looking. They all suddenly heard a loud 'squelch'. Molly and Hugh shot their heads around to discover where the peculiar noise had come from. Their eyes soon fell to the green, squishy substance that was now spread generously across Ally's mum's bum. Hugh and Molly erupted into laughter and their knees buckled as they clutched their stomachs. Their laughter only grew louder as they watched Ally's mum smear her fingers through the cow poo. She remained silent as she unsteadily got to her feet to survey the damage to her clothes. A large piece of cow poo fell off and onto the ground.

Molly attempted to speak but couldn't stop laughing long enough to get the words out. She took in a huge gulp of air to try and supress the laughter, but Hugh beat her to it. "That's a bit like your behaviour towards Mum recently, Grandma," he said cheekily. This then sent Hugh and Molly into another fit of giggles as they watched the realisation dawn on Ally's mum's face.
"Nothing like getting what you give," added Molly with a wink. With that, Hugh and Molly started to run to the top of the hill, laughing as they went.

4 DREAM TEAM

Ally ran her finger down the names on her list, to check that each one had a tick beside it. She flopped gratefully back into the chair. The army of love had been assembled. She allowed a smile of hope to curl her lips and she unconsciously raised her arms up in the air, in celebration. But, her moment was interrupted by a 'clunk' from the hallway. She turned her head to see Billy and Ben walking through the front door. Ally skipped across and proudly placed the sheet of paper down on the kitchen table. "We have help," she announced, still amazed.
Ben wrapped his arms around her and squeezed her tightly. "Well done, Miss Ally," he said in admiration.
"Watch out!" said Billy suddenly. "They are on the return." They all studied the three figures coming

down the hill. Ally immediately snatched up the list and went to hide it in the office desk drawer before returning to Ben and Billy.

"I think your mum may have hurt herself," observed Billy. "She is walking in a really strange way," he added as he continued to watch them make their way to the front door.
Hugh and Molly bounded in first. "Hey, Mum," he said easily as he gave Ally a hug. Molly followed. She had her hand across her mouth and was clearly trying to smother some giggles.
Ben gave her a curious look. "Everything alright there, Molly?" Ben asked. Molly nodded as another giggle escaped through her fingertips.

"Eww, what's that stench?" Ally cried, pinching her nose.
"That would be the smell of prize cattle," declared Billy. "With healthy stomachs." They all then watched Ally's mum stagger in through the front door. Ally opened her mouth to speak but before she could say anything, her mum put up a hand to stop her. They all bit their lips now as the cause of Molly's laughter became very apparent. They stayed silent as they listened to Ally's mum's footsteps disappear upstairs. Molly was the first to surrender and the kitchen soon filled with her infectious laughter. One by one, they all joined in.

"What happened?" Ben managed to splutter

out.

"She said she was tired and wanted to rest, but just sat down without checking," Hugh explained as they both chuckled again.

"Maybe she won't be coming back here again anytime soon," Ally said, wiping away her laughter-tears.

"Let's hope so," Molly replied.

Billy shot Molly a look of disapproval. "Don't you be lowering yourself to her level," he said firmly. They all fell silent. "No, Sir," replied Molly apologetically.

"Right then. I am off out. Be back soon," Ally said as she grabbed the truck keys and her handbag.

"Can I come?" Molly asked with pleading eyes.

"Yes, of course," replied Ally, and Molly followed her out of the house and to the car. They climbed into the truck and pulled down the driveway. Ally held her hand out of the window and let it glide through the air. She could feel herself getting further and further away from her troubles, and the sense of freedom grew bigger. "Are you excited?" asked Molly.

Ally glanced across. "Yes," Ally answered with conviction. "I can't think of any other person I would rather spend the rest of my life with. To be loved, unconditionally, for the person you are, even in the bad times, now that is true love. And that's how Ben makes me feel - whole and complete." Ally pulled out onto the road and headed towards town.

Molly watched the countryside roll on by. "I am glad I got to stay with you," Molly whispered.

Molly felt Ally's hand squeeze hers. "I wasn't going to have it any other way," said Ally tenderly. Ally soon turned left, into the garden centre.

"Are we going to order the flowers?" Molly asked as she sat up taller in her seat.

"Not quite," Ally replied as she pulled into an empty parking space. "Come on. Let me show you," she added as she climbed out of the car.

Molly took hold of Ally's hand as they walked into the garden centre. They were hit by a wave of beautiful flower-scents and an array of colour.

"This way, I think," Ally said as she guided Molly outside. They went through the sliding doors, to the back, where the trees were. There, at the end, stood 3 trees, adorned with pure, white flowers.

"Ah, there we go," stated Ally and she strode purposefully towards them.

"What are they?" Molly asked.

"Cherry blossom trees," Ally said as she carefully surveyed each one, to decide which she would be taking home. "In some cultures," she explained. "This tree represents how overwhelmingly beautiful life is, but also, how short it is. Mother nature's reminder to show up and make the most of the day we have, instead of wishing it away." Ally continued to survey the trees. "That's the one," she said decisively as she moved some pots out of the way and slid the chosen one out.

Molly and Ally each grabbed one side of the pot, and slowly walked with it to the cashier. "Morning, Mam," greeted the cashier. "And is there anything else you would like today?" he asked.
"No, just this," said Ally as she punched in her pin number.
The cashier passed her the receipt. "There you go," he said. "Have a great day!"
"You too," said Ally as she and Molly readjusted their grip and carefully carried the tree to the boot of the truck.
"Here, let me help you with that, Mam," offered a gentleman as he lifted the plant pot into the truck for them.
"Thank you," smiled Ally and she and Molly climbed into the truck. "Help is always there when you need it," Ally said gleefully.

As Ally pulled off and began the drive back, she took in a deep breath. "This tree will be our family tree as we go through the seasons of life together, and weather the stormy days," she said. "Our roots will run deep and strong, and nourish our family. But the branches will each go in their own direction as they grow. Just like you and Hugh going off on your own adventures. It will be a daily reminder to look at what is beautiful about life, and to make the most of the time we have." Ally smiled at Molly.

"I like that," said Molly as she turned to look out of the window.

They eventually arrived back at the house. "Where are you going to put it?" asked Molly as they turned into the driveway and the house came into view.

"Hmm, I'm not quite sure yet?" Ally replied.

"And where are you having the wedding?" queried Molly.

"I don't know that one either," Ally answered with a hint of anxiety.

"And who is going to do the food and the music?" continued Molly. Ally stayed quite still as the mammoth task that lay ahead descended over her. It felt like a dark cloud rolling in and she felt the heaviness of sadness begin to take over.

Ally slowed the truck down and they parked up in front of the house. Ben stepped out to greet them. Molly was the first to jump out and she ran up to give him a hug. "Did you get everything you needed?" asked Ben as he squeezed her tightly. "Yes! Come and look," Molly answered excitedly, and she took his hand. She bounced towards the back of the truck, dragging Ben with her. Ally was already waiting there.

"Here is my something nice," Ally said with a smile.

"It's a blossom tree, and..." Molly chipped in, but before she could continue, Ben patted her on the shoulder.

"I know the story too," he said. "Come on. Let's get it out."

"We just don't know where its home is?" pondered a puzzled Molly, and she scratched her chin like a detective.

Ben smiled a knowing smile. He carried it just a short distance, and placed it right in the centre of the driveway. "Here," he said decisively. "Now we will always be greeted by the tree when we come home. And you can see it from every part of the house. It shall be our guardian," he added as he sunk his hands deep into his pockets. "What do you think, Ally?"

Ally smiled. "It's perfect," she said. Molly suddenly darted across to the barn and then promptly re- appeared with a shovel. Ally walked over to Ben and slid her hand around his back. She rested her head on his shoulder, and for the first time, knew that everything was going to be alright.

"It sure is," whispered Ben.

Ally looked up. "Hey," she chuckled. "Mind reader."

Molly returned with Billy. Hugh wasn't far behind. They all watched Ben begin to dig a hole, but Billy quickly joined in. Ally removed the tree from the pot as Ben surveyed his work. "That should be deep enough," he said as he and Ally lifted the tree into its new home. Molly and Hugh then picked up the shovels and moved the soil back, to cover the roots.

"That looks good," said Billy as he took a step back to get a better look.

Ally slipped her hand into Ben's. "This is where we are going to get married," she announced. They all looked at her.

"That's good for me," Ben confirmed, kissing her sweetly.

Hugh and Molly began to skip around the blossom tree, shouting "yippee," as they danced.

"May I say a few words?" asked Billy as he removed his hat. Ben took his hat off too. "Life, bless this tree with your unconditional love. Let it be a beacon to guide this family through each day and help them remember what is important. Protect and shelter those under it from fear and doubt. And let the sunshine through its branches to fill each one of us with hope and courage. May this family's roots run deep and strong, and enable us to weather any storm. Stand tall and strong so we can do too. And let you be our reminder to stop and take a moment of gratitude each day, for the beauty of life, until our last breath."

"Amen, amen," they all responded.

Ally walked up to Billy and hugged him. "Thank you," she whispered sweetly.

"Right. Well, I best be hitting the road," said Billy as he shuffled uncomfortably. He placed his hat firmly back on his head, sunk his hands deep into his pockets and walked, head down, to his truck.

"I best make a start on dinner," said Ally and they all made their way across to the front door. They stepped into the silence and filed straight into the kitchen.

"It's spookily silent," noticed Hugh as he glanced up at the ceiling. "I wonder if Grandma is OK," he added as he got goose bumps.

"How about you take her up a cup of tea, and let her know that dinner will be in half an hour," Ally said as she flicked the switch on the kettle. She headed to the fridge to get the milk and a Shepherd's Pie that she had made the previous day.

Hugh reached for a mug and he and Molly manoeuvred around each other as they set the table and made tea. "I'll come up with you," Molly said as she watched Hugh carefully lift the mug and shuffle his feet tentatively across the floor. Ally placed the Shepherd's Pie in the oven and Ben poured two glasses of wine. He motioned for Ally to follow him out onto the back porch. They sat down on the bench and watched the sun begin to set behind the mountain. Ally snuggled in closer and felt the warmth of Ben's body radiate and absorb into hers.

Ben slipped his hand into his jeans pocket, pulled out two wedding bands and placed them in Ally's hand. "These were my grandma's and grandpa's," he said. "I would like us to use them for our wedding bands. There are many years of unconditional love woven into these two rings. And before my grandma passed, she sat me down and told me the story of when my grandpa asked her to marry him. It wasn't a fairy tale story, but the lesson in it is something that has guided me through a lot of my decisions. She told me that life rarely says no to our wishes, but it does ask you to have the courage to say 'yes', and even though fear may be telling you not to take one more step forwards, that's when you need to move forwards the most. She told me that we are all worthy of our dreams coming true, but that you have to make sure you are ready to say 'yes' to receiving them, when the opportunity arrives."

Ally rolled the rings around in between her fingers, and then clasped them tightly in the palm of her hand. Her gaze drifted up to Ben. "I am ready to receive," she said confidently. They raised their glasses as the sunset turned the sky into a swirling pool of reds, yellows and oranges - a firework of colour. The 'chink' of their glasses rang through the silent valley.

Ally and Ben sat in silence, speaking beyond words. As the blanket of the night sky was pulled across, the squeak of the door brought them out of their trance. "Ally, I think dinner is ready," said Molly gently. But there was a sudden eruption of noise – the unmistakable sound of a wooden spoon being hit against an empty pan and Hugh's voice shouting, "DINNER TIME!" Molly rolled her eyes and Ben and Ally chuckled as they got up and headed inside.

They all sat around the table in easy silence. Ally's mum was wearing a fresh set of clothes. The only sound to be heard was knives and forks being scraped against now empty plates. "Right," said Ally to Hugh and Molly. "You two monkeys, shower and then bed. I need you all recharged and ready for tomorrow." She collected the empty plates and passed them to Ben, who put them in the dishwasher.

"Why? What's happening tomorrow?" asked Molly with a hint of excitement.

"I'll tell you when the sun rises," Ally said with a cheeky grin.

"Oh, come on! Please," begged Molly.

"Bed!" said Ally firmly as she pointed her finger towards the living room.

Ben closed the dishwasher door. "Right then, you two," he said as he ran towards Hugh and Molly, causing them both to scamper towards the stairs.

"I think I will turn in as well," said Ally's mum wearily, as she stiffly got up from her chair. "I think I have had enough excitement for one day." Ben stepped aside and he watched Ally's mum parade to her room. Ally made herself a cup of tea and began to make her way to bed, too. Ben wasn't far behind.

"Ally, Ally! Wake up! The sun has risen," Molly squealed as she threw back the curtains and illuminated the room with bright, morning sunlight. "Now can you tell me?" she asked as she leapt up onto the bed.

Ally hoisted herself into an upright position whilst Ben continued to sleep through the commotion. Ally wearily rubbed her face with her hands. It was going to be a tough few days. Was she ready for it? "Today should be the day that the cavalry arrive," Ally explained, forcing a smile.

Molly dropped to her knees. "Really?" she cried. "Everyone is coming here?" she asked with wide eyed excitement.

Ally nodded. "Yep, the army of love."

Molly rolled onto her back. "I like the sound of that," she said. "Maybe Mum and Dad can help too, from the stars."

Ally gently rubbed Molly's hair. "I am sure they are pulling out all the stops, to help us," she said reassuringly.

"Can you go and get Hugh, please?" asked Ally gently.

"HUGH!" Molly screamed, and Ally rolled her eyes.

Ben stirred. "Good morning, Foghorn," he mumbled as he propped himself up and leant his head on his hand. Molly chuckled.

It wasn't long before Hugh bounded down the hallway and ran into the bedroom. He jumped onto the bed, squishing Molly. "Agh, get off, Hugh, you great, big buffalo," she ordered.

Ben began to tickle them both. "You are two cheeky monkeys!" he giggled as they squirmed under his fingertips.

"Alright. Everyone settle down. It's family meeting time," announced Ally. "We all need to pull together. This house is going to get very busy for the next few days, and that means you two need to get to bed on time, and when asked to do something by one of the adults, there is no arguing - just complete the task. Ben, you're in charge of parking everyone up today. Just make sure it's away from the blossom tree. I need to pop into town to get something. So, Molly and Hugh, I need you to tidy your bedrooms and then make a start on breakfast," she said.

Ally turned to Ben. "I'll go and set up the area next to the barn, for everyone to park," he said. "They can hook up to the electric in the barn." His eyes sparkled with excitement. It was the same look that Ally and Hugh had when they followed him back to the ranch for the first time.

"Right then, troops. Onwards and upwards," Ally declared, throwing back the duvet.

"One team! One dream!" Hugh said, leaping to his feet and punching the air.

Hugh and Molly ran to tidy their rooms. "Bet I can get it done before you!" teased Molly.

Ally made her way towards the bathroom. "What are you going into town for?" asked Ben as his feet hit the floor and he tried to wake up his tired body.

Ally turned around and winked. "You'll see," she replied mischievously as she slowly closed the bathroom door.

The house filled with the sound of thundering

feet down the stairs as Molly and Hugh moved onto their next task of getting breakfast ready. They were soon joined by Ben and Ally's mum in the kitchen. Polite words were spoken between them as Ben attempted to keep a conversation flowing, but the atmosphere was charged. An oncoming thunderstorm was building inside of Ally's mum. Ben couldn't hide his look of relief when he saw Billy's truck pull up. Ben watched Billy walk in through the front door but then pause as he saw the back of Ally's mum's head. "Let me get you a coffee," Ben said quickly as he saw his dad clearly planning his escape route.

Billy surrendered and took a seat at the kitchen table. Molly took a mouthful of cereal and raised her eyebrows at Billy. "I'll see everyone in a bit," announced Ally as she waltzed into the kitchen. She picked up a travel mug filled with tea, which Hugh had kindly made for her.
"Why?" quizzed Ally's mum. "Where are you off to, young lady?"
"Thanks for the compliment, Mum. That anti-aging cream must be working a treat," Ally remarked before disappearing out of the front door.

"Well, where is she off to?" repeated Ally's mum, turning to scowl at each person around the table. No one said a word as they shrugged their shoulders in response. "Well it's good to know you all talk to each other," Ally's mum said sarcastically as she got up from her chair. "I am going to tend to my correspondence," she added before marching back up the stairs.

Billy couldn't help himself and he let out a long sigh as she left the room. Ben stood up. "Right, time to get ready for everyone arriving," he said. "John sent me a text to say that they are about an hour away."
Billy stood up and placed his hat on his head with a firm push. "I'll keep going with that job list. And I guess you'll be needing the extra cables for the trailers?" Ben nodded.
"We'll sort out the horses this morning and do the feeding and mucking out," Molly said as she collected the plates.
Ben pretended to collapse against the worktop in disbelief. "Molly! You must make sure I'm sitting down before you tell me things like that," he chuckled.

Molly playfully hit him with a towel. "Haven't you got work to do?" she asked with a smile.
The three of them lined up in front of Molly. "Aye-aye, Captain," they chorused with a salute before marching out the front door. Molly quickly put the plates down and skipped on behind. Molly and Hugh pulled on their now, well-worn boots and

ran across to the barn. Molly walked past each of the stalls, rubbing the horse's noses as she went. "Good morning, Red Rock. Good morning, Firefly. Good morning..." Molly suddenly stopped. "Hugh, come quick and take a look at this," she said. Hugh sprinted down to where Molly was standing. And there in front of them, was a brown and white patched horse. It walked across to the stable door and ruffled Molly's hair with its nose, causing Molly to laugh.

"Who is this? When did it arrive?" Hugh asked. He looked at Molly, wild eyed with excitement.
"I don't know, but let's find out," she replied. They ran outside and around the side of the barn to where Ben was standing.
"Whose is the new horse? Whose is the new horse?" they chanted in unison.
"Well, you two don't miss a trick," chuckled Ben, without looking up. "It's a gift for Ally," he explained.
"I didn't know Ally rode?" Molly said.
Hugh shuffled uncomfortably. "She did, before Dad died," he explained sadly. "But then after that, she lost interest."
Ben stepped across and wrapped his arm around Hugh. "Well, I was thinking that we may just have to change that," Hugh said. "As I think it would be nice for us to, once in a while, pack up the saddle

bags with a picnic, and all go out for a ride across the land. With your mum riding Wildfire," Ben added with a smile.

"That would be so amazing!" Molly cried, jumping in the air like a rocket.
"But, you've got to keep it a secret," Ben said firmly, turning to them both.
Hugh and Molly put their hands across their hearts. "We promise," they said in allegiance.
"We'll just make sure it's got plenty of hay and water," said Ben. "We can then close the barn door when the rest of the horses have gone out, and it can stretch its legs around the barn whilst we muck out," he added as Billy arrived with the extension cable and some posts.

Molly and Hugh ran back into the barn and settled into their new routine. Molly made the feeds and Hugh took them to the stables. Molly then haltered up Firefly and Red Rock whilst Hugh got two of the ranch horses. They then led them all out to the field. They sprinted back to the barn, the thrill and excitement fuelling their footsteps. As Molly and Hugh pulled the barn door closed, they ran towards Wildfire's stable. They opened up the door, and Hugh grabbed his morning feed and put it out in the aisle. Wildfire casually walked out. His legs were long, mostly white but with a few brown patches splashed across his skin. He had a pink nose and kind eyes. As he nuzzled the food and began to eat, Molly ran her fingers across his hair. "It's like silk," she whispered.

Hugh put his hand on Wildfire's shoulder. "He's beautiful," he agreed. "Mom is going to love him." A peaceful feeling descended over him. A feeling of times yet to come and of new memories yet to be made. "Come on, we best get mucking out before Aden arrives," Hugh said, breaking out of his trance. Molly reluctantly stepped away from Wildfire. She groaned as she went to get the wheelbarrow. Hugh got two forks and they made their way to the first stable.

They both set to mucking out, but suddenly felt a presence behind them. Molly turned around and was greeted by Wildfire, nose to nose. He was holding his now empty feed bucket in his mouth. "Wildfire, you scared me," Molly said, jumping back.
Hugh cautiously took the feed bowl from Wildfire's mouth. "Thank you," he said. And then looked on in amazement as Wildfire backed out of the stable, walked across to where the bales of hay were stacked, and started to munch.

Molly and Hugh looked at each other. "I wonder if he knows anymore cool tricks," Hugh said eagerly. Just then, they heard a campervan.

"Helen and Bill are here," Hugh cried as he
dropped his fork and ran to the barn door.
"Hey!" shouted Molly. "Don't leave me with all the
mucking out!" But Hugh had already disappeared
outside. She let out a long sigh.
Hugh sprinted in the direction of the sound of the
engine. Bill was just pulling up to one of the areas
that Ben had marked out. Bill wound down the
window. "Well, look at you," he said, beaming at
Hugh.
Helen then stepped out of the van and Hugh ran
around to give her a big hug. "Hello, Hugh,"
greeted Helen.
"I've got so much to tell you," Hugh said joyously.
"We can't wait to hear about all your adventures,"
said Bill as he came around to join in the hug.
"But first, let us get set up and started on what
needs to be done. And then you can fill us in on
all that is new," he added warmly. Just then, they
saw a shadow of a girl walking towards them. It
was Molly. As she got closer, she took out her
locket and began to twiddle it between her
fingers. The butterflies in her stomach began to
multiply.

Bill broadened his smile.
"This is Molly, the newest member to our family,"
said Ben who had stepped up beside her.
Molly smiled cautiously. "Hi," she whispered.
Helen moved forwards and wrapped Molly in a

warm hug. "Hi, Molly. It's a pleasure to meet you," she said warmly as her eyes sparkled. Molly felt herself soften and relax as Helen enveloped her with love.

Bill held out his hand. "Mam," he said as Molly took hold and gave it a firm shake. Bill took back his hand and stretched out his fingers. "That's a strong grip you've got there," he said with a wink, shaking his hand.

Hugh took hold of Molly's hand. "Come on," he said sneakily. "We've got 'you know what' to sort out," and he nodded towards the barn. They both ran back to finish off their chores.

Bill clapped his hands together. "Right, what can we do?"

"Umm," replied Ben hesitantly, shuffling from side to side. "Well, I'm not too sure. Ally's the one with the job list and she had to go into town," Ben said. But, just as the words were leaving his mouth, he saw Ally driving down the driveway.

Ben waved to signal for Ally to come over. She drove round and parked next to Ben's trailer. As she stepped out, her heartbeat grew faster as she saw a familiar and much-welcome sight.

"You're here!" she cried, unable to hide the relief in her voice.

"Where else would we be," said Bill as he walked over to Ally and hugged her tightly.

"You looking amazing," breathed Helen, pushing Bill aside to get her turn at hugging Ally. An atmosphere of excitement and love began to shine.

"I'll go and put the kettle on," said Ally and she motioned for them to follow her to the house.

"And show us this job list of yours," Bill remarked. Ally blushed.

"Pa! Take a break and come and have a coffee," Ben shouted as Billy appeared from behind Ben's workshop. Molly and Hugh heard their voices as they all made their way to the house. They led Wildfire back into his stable, complete with a clean bed, fresh hay and water. "We'll be back again later," soothed Molly as she rubbed his nose. When they stepped into the house, they were hit with a wave of excitement. Helen, Ally, Bill, Billy and Ben were all sitting around the kitchen table, with fresh coffee and tea, and lots of animated chat.

Ally laid out a piece of paper in the centre of the table. But they were interrupted by a truck and trailer pulling up outside the house. "Aden is here!" cried Hugh, running to the door.

"Can you show them where to park," called Ben behind him. Hugh just caught his words on the wind as he ran past John's truck, waving with his arms for them to follow him. He sprinted past the barn, towards Bill's campervan. John obediently followed, and pulled up at the next post along. Sally and Aden stepped out. "Hi, Hugh," said Sally.

Hugh bounced up and down, unable to contain his excitement any longer. "Come on over to the house," he said eagerly. "We are all in the kitchen." He signalled towards the door as John stepped out of the truck. Hugh and Aden sprinted ahead, followed by John and Sally.

Ally got up to put the kettle back on. "Hi, everyone," greeted Sally as she stepped through the door. Bill and Helen got up to hug them both. Ben stood up and shook John's hand. "Good to see you again, John," he said with a smile. Molly walked across to hug Aden and they all got rearranged around the table. Bill sat back down and took out his reading glasses. He scanned down the list. "So, when do we have to have this done by?" he asked. "Saturday," Ally replied, sounding a little deflated at the prospect. Bill peered over the top of his glasses. "It wasn't the date I picked," Ally whispered, as they all heard the sound of a bedroom door closing and footsteps coming down the stairs.

Ally's mum appeared at the kitchen doorway. "Everyone," said Ally. "This is my mum." They all felt the sudden change in the atmosphere, and offered a series of awkward 'hellos', nods and raised cups.

"When is Jane arriving?" Ally's mum asked in a new tone of voice.

"She flies in tomorrow," Ally said, handing her mum a cup of tea.

"And where will she sleep? The couch?" Ally's mum asked with disgust in her voice.

"No, in Ben's trailer," Ally explained as she felt the happiness begin to leak out of her body.

"Well, that's no way to treat your oldest friend," remarked her mum rudely.

"Well, it's good enough for us," John said protectively. Ally's mum stared at John, like a bull preparing to charge, before heading out to go and sit on the back porch.

"She's something alright," John said sipping his tea. "Oh, Ally," he said dreamily. "I sure have missed your cups of tea." Sally rolled her eyes.

"Tom and Chad will be arriving tomorrow as well," Ben said. "Then the rest of the guests who have been invited will arrive on the day."

"Invited by who?" Helen asked naively. Ben stayed quiet.

"By my mum" Ally explained with bitterness in her voice.

Bill reached across and squeezed Ally's hand reassuringly. "There will always be a fly in the ointment," he said. "No matter how hard we try.

But, it doesn't need to spoil anything," he encouraged.

"Well then. Bill, you get cracking on that list," instructed Helen. "And I will rustle us something up for lunch," she added as she tapped him on the shoulder.

"Let's take a look at that list there, Bill," John said as he and Sally scanned the jobs. "We'll make a start on setting out the chairs and hanging up the fairy lights," said John.

"I'll keep on with the repairs," added Billy.

"I'll give you a hand with that," Bill offered.

Ben turned to Molly, Hugh and Aden. "You three. Can you please go round each of the paddocks to check that there are no broken rails, that the waters are clean, and that the horses and cattle have enough food?" They all nodded eagerly.

"Then you can do evening chores later on," Ben added.

Everyone got to their feet and began to make their way out of the front door. The hum of conversation filled the air, like birds serenading a glorious day. Ben stepped across to Ally who was busy stacking the dishwasher. He took hold of her hand and began to dance with her around the kitchen. "We are so lucky," Ally said smiling up at him.

"It's all going to be alright, Miss Ally," Ben said

gently. "No need to worry anymore." He gently dipped her backwards causing her to laugh.
"I know," she said. "It's just that dark cloud that I wish would go," she added, motioning towards the back porch.
"Her daughter is getting married. She will smile at some point," whispered Ben, before twirling Ally around once more and then making his way to the front door.

He opened the door to find Helen standing there, arms laden with food bags. Ben stepped to the side to let her through. "Right then," said Helen. "I thought I'd make a chilli to serve up when everyone gets hungry." She plonked the food bags down on the table.
"Helen, you're an angel!" Ally cried as she realised that she hadn't even thought about food.

They began to prepare the food as they watched the throng of people moving forwards and backwards in front of the house. Sally balanced on a ladder, covering the front porch with lights and little jars filled with yellow roses. Molly, Hugh and Aden carried the chairs that Sally and John had brought with them, and placed them next to the new blossom tree. They then headed out to check the pastures. Billy and Bill were busy driving around in the truck, stopping to mend any broken gates or railings. Ben kept dipping in and out of view near the barn as he sorted out the last necessities for their new campers.

Ally leaned against the side of the worktop with a fresh cup of tea in her hand. She watched the whirlwind of love transform the house, and all of her little ideas come together. Ally's mum returned from the back porch, took Ally's fresh cup of tea out of her hands and sat down with it at the kitchen table. Ally sighed as she turned the kettle back on. "It all looks busy out there," Ally's mum stated. "But don't you think you should get married in a church and have a proper service?" she scoffed. Helen glanced across at Ally who gave a weak smile. "And those lights. Don't you think you should have real candles? It looks so cheap," Ally's mum continued, and her words began to unpick Ally's dream, stitch by stitch. "Haven't you got important people to e-mail, or something?" Ally asked, praying she would leave her alone.
"No. I have caught up with everything I needed to," replied her mum. "Which leaves me able to help you before this turns out to be a disaster." Ally's mum smirked as she took a sip of tea.

Ally's eyes widened in horror as she looked pleadingly at Helen. Helen wiped her hands on a towel. "How about we go into town and get the food supplies for the day," Helen suggested to Ally's mum. "Do you know what you are having?" Helen asked Ally. But Ally was looking blankly back at her. "Well, if you wouldn't mind, I'd love to cook the food for the big day," Helen said with a twinkle in her eye.

Ally stepped across, hugged Helen and whispered, "thank you," with unshakable gratitude. "Mum, could you organise some wine and soft drinks too," Ally said, trying to create things to keep her mum occupied.

"I will just go and get my things," Ally's mum said as she got up from the table and disappeared upstairs.

Helen looked into Ally's eyes. "Remember, Ally. There comes a point when your choices aren't about your parents and what they would like, but about you and your life. It's your parent's role to raise you and give you the best start, but it's your job to evolve what you have learnt, and to grow and discover new things. This teaches parents new perspectives, new ways of doing things, and keeps things moving forwards."

Ally looked down. "I know," she replied. "It's just so hard though, when you feel that your suggestions aren't being listened to or that they are being rejected just because they are different from tradition," she explained with a heavy heart.

"Even a tradition was something new when it was carried out for the first time," Helen said, squeezing Ally's shoulder.

Ally's mum reappeared. "Right, shall we go?" she asked as she strode to the front door. "Wish me luck," whispered Helen with a wink as she followed Ally's mum outside.

5 FINDING THE TRUTH IN OUR FEARS

Billy and Bill stepped into an empty kitchen but they could smell the succulent, fresh chilli. Bill's stomach rumbled. "Ah, food," he said, breathing in deeply.

"Coffee?" Billy asked as he waved a mug in the air. Bill nodded. He glanced around, looking for signs of Helen or Ally. He noticed the office light was on, and made his way across.

He peered through the door and gently tapped on the frame with his fingers. Ally swung around and greeted him with a broad smile.

"How's the list going?" Bill asked.

"Shrinking quickly," Ally said with obvious relief.

"Many hands make light work," Bill acknowledged. "May I?" he asked politely, motioning to come in.

"Of course," said Ally. Bill stepped in and perched

on the edge of the desk.

"What's next on the list for us to do?" he
asked as he glanced down at the page.
"Food!" Ally exclaimed just as her stomach gave
an obvious rumble.
"I think that's one of my favourite jobs on the
list!" laughed Bill. They stepped out of the office
and Ally went to ring the bell on the front porch,
to herald everyone back to the house. She then
placed Helen's chilli in the centre of the kitchen
table with some bread and a big pan of rice.

Bill dived in, straight away, and his mouth
began to water at the tempting smell. As the
truck pulled up outside, Bill saw Helen and he
quickly scampered into the living room with his
plate. Ally watched and sniggered. Bill put his
finger to his lips. "Shh, don't tell Helen," he said
playfully.

"What smells so good?" Molly asked as she
walked into the kitchen.
"Helen's finest cooking," Ally stated as she
handed Molly a plate.
Just then, Ben arrived. "You know what?" he said
with a smile on his face. "We might just be ready
on time. I can't believe how much we've got done
already," he said as he leant against the side of
the worktop next to Ally.

Ally absent-mindedly rested her head on Ben's shoulder as she gazed out of the window at the blossom tree. "Which reminds me," she said. "We have sold all of the knives that you have made."
Ben looked at Ally in shock. "Really?" he asked. She nodded proudly. "So, I would suggest that you get back in that workshop, as soon as possible. The orders are growing each day."
Ben ran his fingers through his hair in disbelief. "You should hear the comments people are putting on the website too," continued Ally. She took out her phone and scrolled down the website page to show Ben the testimonials.

"Well...umm...that's really kind of them," said Ben, clearly blushing.
Ally kissed him on the cheek. "The gifts just keep on coming," she sighed. "I think we are being very well rewarded for all that we have been through." Ben looked around at the gathering of people, and the transformations to the house, and the smiles. "I think we are being blessed in ways we could never have even imagined."

Later, they were all sitting around the big table on the back porch, looking out over the vast land. Bill leant back in his chair and his stomach protruded with satisfaction. "Well, I think we could get a few more of those jobs done, but then it will be an early night for me," he said as he stretched his arms above his head.

Helen got up and started to collect all the plates. "I'll get the camper set up," she confirmed as she carried some of the plates through.

Sally did the same. "I'll go and get ours ready too," she said, looking at John, who nodded his agreement.

"Right then, Billy. What's next?" Bill asked as he patted him on the arm.

Billy turned to Ben. "Well, while we have the man power, we might as well sort out those new water drinkers, to clear out some of the clutter next to the barn." Ben nodded at Billy in agreement.

"I'll give a hand too," offered John. "And you three best come as well," he added, looking at Molly, Aden and Hugh.

Ally collected the remaining plates and carried them into the kitchen. "Leave them, love," said Helen kindly. "Me and your mum will sort this out," she added as she handed another dish to Ally's mum, who reluctantly dried it with a towel. Ally graciously accepted and disappeared into the office once more.

The office gradually began to get darker so Ally turned on the office light. She listened to a herd of footsteps crossing the living room floor as everybody began to settle in for the night. There was a knock on the door. "We'll see you in the morning," Sally said as she popped her head round. Ally swirled around in her chair and looked at Sally. "Thank you so much for all your help today," she said warmly. "I can't believe how much has been done," she added gratefully.

"The best is yet to come," Sally said, smiling proudly. "It's about time you had a day to celebrate."
Ally glanced down at her feet. It had been a long year of trials, with very few triumphs. It would be nice to balance the scales a bit. "I have you all here," she said. "Now that is definitely worth celebrating."

Ally watched as Sally, John, Aden, Helen and Billy all walked out the door. "Right, you two. Shower and bed," Ben said to Hugh and Molly, who were standing in the living room, clearly exhausted. They dragged their tired bodies to the stairs. They didn't need much encouragement this evening.
"I think I will be doing the same," said Ally's mum. "Night, all," she added as she followed Molly and Hugh.
Ben raised his eyebrows at Ally. "I'll just go and do final checks and meet you upstairs," he said as he slipped his coat on and disappeared outside.

Ally closed the lid down on her laptop. "That'll do for today," she said to herself as a sense of calm washed over her. She got up, made herself a cup of tea and staggered up the stairs. She looked in on Hugh who was already nestled in his bed. "Night-night, Monkey," she whispered. "Night, Mom," he replied wearily. Ally heard the front door open and close, and the sound of Ben's boot dropping to the floor. She then made her way to Molly's room. "Night-night, Miss Molly." "Night-night, Ally," Molly yawned, fighting to keep her eyes open.

Ally made her way into her bedroom and the sight of the comfy bed was a welcome one indeed. She changed into her pyjamas, climbed in and took a sip of tea. As she placed her mug on her bedside table, she felt her body melt into the mattress and she surrendered to the weight of her eyelids. Ben padded quietly into the room and got changed too. He looked across at Ally who was now fast asleep. He spotted the full cup of tea beside her. "You must have been tired," he whispered as he climbed in next to her and turned out the light.

Molly stared up at the stars and moonlight that were beginning to fade. She quietly crept out of bed and made her way to Hugh's bedroom. She slowly opened the door and slid in under the duvet, next to Hugh. "Hugh, are you awake?" she whispered but the room remained silent. She jabbed her elbow into his side.

"Agh!" cried Hugh, rubbing his ribs.

"Good, you're awake," said Molly. "I can't sleep. My head won't go quiet."

"My head is saying sleep," Hugh replied.

"How can you?" questioned Molly. "It's all so exciting." She squirmed underneath the duvet covers.

Hugh gave in. He knew it was pointless trying to get anymore sleep for the moment. "OK. OK, I'm awake. What do you want to talk about?" he asked, rolling over towards her.

Molly let out a big yawn. "Oh, nothing," she muttered and promptly dropped off to sleep.

Hugh rolled his eyes in the darkness as he settled back down again.

Ally's eyelids fluttered against the morning sunlight and she took in a deep breath. Her lungs filled with the smell of food. "Mmm, what's that smell?" she asked, rolling over, but Ben wasn't there. She looked back at the clock on her bedside table and spotted a note with her name on it, and a gift box with a green ribbon tied around it.

To Miss Ally,

You are the greatest gift I have received from life.

Your love fills me with joy each morning, like a beautiful sunrise. The way you hold this family together is admirable. You are so unique, yet perfect. I have been blessed with such riches to get to spend the rest of my life with you. Here is a little something to lay next to your heart.

Love Ben x

Ally lowered the note and wiped a tear of happiness from the corner of her eye. She reached for the box and opened it. There, inside, lay a locket with a tree carved intricately on the front. She opened it up and saw a photo of herself, Ben, Hugh and Molly in front of the house. And on the left hand side the words: '*My whole world, Ben x*'.

Ally fastened the locket around her neck and climbed out of bed. She got dressed as quickly as she could and ran downstairs. She found Ben at the cooker, and a plate full of bacon and sausages, slices of bread and fresh pots of tea and coffee in the middle of the table. Ally flung her arms around Ben. "Thank you," she whispered.

Molly and Hugh had followed the thundering sound of Ally's footsteps. "Hey, you two," complained Hugh. "No kissing in the morning! I haven't eaten yet," he added as he pretended to be sick.

"Stop being silly, Hugh. It's wonderful," Molly said dreamily as she shepherded Hugh towards a chair.

"Something smells good," shouted Bill as he stepped through the front door. Ally slowly peeled herself off Ben, wishing they could have had a little more time alone together. Ben gave her a wink of agreement. "Just a little something to set us up for the day," Ben said as he placed a plate of eggs on the table too.

"Can me, Molly and Aden go off exploring today?" Hugh asked with a mouthful of breakfast sandwich.

"Not today, Monkey," answered Ally. "We need every pair of available hands, to get ready for tomorrow," she explained, sipping her tea.

"But what on earth is there left to do?" Hugh asked in protest. Ally pulled out an A4 sheet of paper and Hugh's mouth dropped open. "More jobs," he mouthed. Ally nodded silently.

"But, first things first," said Ally. "You can come with me to pick Jane up. She will be so excited to see you."

"Can I come too," Molly asked, swinging her legs under the table.

"Of course," replied Ally. "And Aden as well, if he fancies a trip out. We can stop and pick up ice-creams on the way back," Ally said with a smile. "Well, if I must," sighed Hugh cheekily. "Because it would be rude not to eat ice cream...erm...I mean see Jane," he added, laughing at this own joke.

"Morning, all," said John as he, Sally and Aden joined the kitchen table. John picked up the A4 sheet of paper. "Are theses our orders for today?" he said with a wink.

"Hey!" Sally said, nudging him in the side. "It's Ally's day. She can have anything she wants," she added, sitting down next to Ally.

Ally's mum appeared, causing everyone to go silent. "I'll be waiting in the truck," she said directly at Helen before turning on her heels and marching out.

Helen nodded with a smile. "I'll be with you in a minute," she said, getting up from her seat. Ally looked apologetically at Helen. "Don't worry," Helen said reassuringly. "I'm enjoying the time with your mum. She is a really nice lady."

Ally looked confused. "You must not be talking about Grandma," Hugh piped up.

Helen looked at Hugh. "Young man, you'll soon learn that her biting words aren't because she wants to hurt you. It's because she loves you and is afraid. Your grandma has her reasons for her actions and words." Hugh remained silent and Ally continued to look confused. Helen placed her hand on Ally's shoulder and gave it a squeeze before heading out the front door.

Billy was the next to arrive and he promptly sat down at the table to make himself a breakfast sandwich. He picked up the A4 sheet and scanned the list. "Chad and Tom should be here by lunchtime," Ben said, handing Billy a coffee. "We best get a move on," said Ally taking a last sip of tea and getting up from the table.
"Aden, do you want to come and get ice cream?" Hugh asked excitedly.
Molly rolled her eyes. "You mean pick Jane up," she corrected. Aden looked across at Sally for approval and she nodded her agreement.
"Yes!" said Aden as he jumped to his feet.

"We'll see you soon," Ally said, giving Ben a quick kiss before they all whooshed out of the door.
"Ah, peace," Billy said, pouring himself another cup of coffee as he felt the atmosphere begin to calm.
Ben joined him at the table. "I'll just need to go into my workshop for a few hours this morning, then we can finish this list off," Ben said, motioning towards the sheet of paper.
"Sounds good to me," John acknowledged.
Ben left the house and he glanced at the blossom tree as he passed. A smile of joy curled his

mouth. He headed towards his workshop, opened the door and flipped the light switch on. There, on the centre of his work bench, was a brown box. He placed his coffee down next to it and lifted the lid. He found a tooled, leather belt with images of the countryside, trees, mountains, a flowing river and an eagle flying in the sky engraved into the leather. The belt had a silver buckle with a stag and deer's head in the centre. He rolled the belt over and, engraved on the back of the buckle, were the words: *'With eternal love, Ally* x'.

Ben took in a deep breath and beamed a smile which lit up the whole workshop. He slipped off his old belt, lay it in the box and put on his new one. "The gifts just keep on coming," he said as he swayed his hips. The sunlight glinted off his new buckle. He sat down, pulled a knife handle towards him and began to engrave.

Ally zoomed down the road. She tapped her fingers on the steering wheel in time to the music as her excitement began to grow. She couldn't wait to show Jane her new life. Molly looked over at her from the passenger seat, and caught sight of the locket which lay around Ally's neck. She lifted hers out from under her jumper, so that it lay in just the same way. Ally ducked in and out of the traffic and finally saw the 'Arrivals' sign for the airport in the distance. "Are you excited?"

asked Molly through gritted teeth as she grabbed the door handle against the swerving, yet again. "Very!" said Ally, her eyes wide and fixed to the road. The car began to slow as Ally took the slip road into the arrivals area. There, by the curb, under the sign, stood a familiar figure. Hugh reached forwards between the two front seats and started pressing the car horn. 'Honk, honk!" He waved vigorously with the other hand.

Ally pulled the truck alongside where Jane was standing and they all climbed out. "Oh my goodness," cried Jane. "You are so tall now," she said, squeezing Hugh and Molly at the same time. "And you are radiant," she added, pulling Ally into a warm, bear-hug.
"Oh, I have missed you," Ally replied as she melted into the hug.
"This is our friend, Aden," interrupted Molly politely. Jane gave him a squeeze too and everyone jumped back into the truck.
"So, what have you all got to tell me?" asked Jane. "We'll discuss 'you know who' later," she added, raising her eyebrows up at Ally.

"You should see the house!" Molly said dreamily. "It is so beautiful."
"And everyone is there, too," Hugh added with a big smile.
"Which reminds me," said Ally. "We just need to

make one stop first, to pick up flowers."
"Oh...but," Hugh said, looking disheartened. Ally
glanced at him in the rear view mirror, a knowing
look on her face. Hugh sank back silently into his
seat.

"It's all coming together," explained Ally.
"And, miraculously, I think we may just be ready
for tomorrow." She was even surprised at her
own words.
"Well, this isn't what I was expecting," replied
Jane with open admiration. "I thought you'd all be
pulling your hair out, stressed and shouting."
"That's not how our family does things," said
Molly, looking out of the window. "We make any
dream come true."
Ally soon pulled in front of a shop, surrounded by
flowers. "Back in a minute," she said, hopping out
of the car and disappearing into the shop.

Jane turned around in her seat. "Tell me
honestly," she said earnestly. "How have things
been? How is your grandma?"
"Weirdly OK," answered Hugh. "She was really
annoying when she arrived, and she upset Mum.
But, since then, she has made friends with Helen
and she has been alright," he explained with a
shrug.
"Ally seems strangely calm about all of this,"
added Molly.

"Well, let me know if I can help you three in any way," offered Jane kindly. "I can't wait to see the house. Will you show me around?" she asked eagerly.

"Yes! Definitely," they all said just as Ally got back into the truck. She handed a small tub of ice-cream to Molly, Hugh and Aden. A group of people loaded the truck boot with flowers. One of the women waved to signal that they had finished.

"Thank you," Ally said, leaning her head out of the window.

"Right then," said Ally decisively. "Let's get back and see what's left to be done." She started up the truck and pulled out onto the road. Jane remained silent as she absorbed the vast view, and the small town with the row of shops. Ally turned at the traffic light and headed out, further into the countryside, before turning into their driveway. "Well, this is home now," Ally announced, glancing across at Jane.

"Wow! I think you have definitely landed on your feet, Ally. This place is gorgeous!" Jane said in amazement.

Ally blushed. "Hey! Tom and Chad are here," Hugh said, pointing at the extra trailer. Ally pulled in front of the house and Molly, Hugh and Aden leapt out to find the new arrivals.

Jane and Ally both glanced up and saw Ally's mum standing on the front porch. "Oh my," Jane muttered and they cautiously climbed out of the truck.

"Oh, Jane," gushed Ally's mum. "How wonderful that you are here." She floated down the steps and kissed Jane on both cheeks. "Ally, take Jane's things to Ben's trailer whilst I make her a cup of tea," she ordered.

Jane looked behind her and mouthed the word 'sorry' before being herded in through the front door.

"Let me help you with that," said a soft voice behind Ally. She turned to find Ben standing there and lifting out Jane's suitcase.

"And so it begins," sighed Ally with a heavy heart.

"Ally, this is your home. Which means you get a say in what happens," Ben said encouragingly.

Ally automatically touched her new locket. "Hey, handsome, nice belt," she said proudly, feeling a little brighter.

"A wonderful woman gave it to me," replied Ben, wiggling his bum as he walked.

Ally marched into the house, interrupting her mum's grand talk as she showed Jane around. Helen smiled warmly at Jane as she unpacked the shopping bags. "And this is the living room," Ally's mum said, a little more loudly, to regain

Jane's attention.

"How about that cup of tea?" Jane suggested, trying to regain a margin of control over the situation.

Ally stood at the front door. "This was my moment, my time to show Jane and she took it from me," she said to herself. She blinked slowly, pushing back the tears and the lump that was forming in her throat.

Helen took a break from the unpacking, walked across to Ally and ushered her into the office. She slowly closed the door behind them. "Is everything OK?" she asked gently.

"Yes," Ally said weakly, but not very convincingly. "I feel like a little school girl and that the school bully just took my friend away," Ally explained, feeling pathetic.

"Good job this is a big house, with plenty to see then," soothed Helen. "How about you take Jane and show her where she will be sleeping, and the outside parts of the house. I'm sure your mum will not be wanting a repeat of the other day. And we will make a start on preparing the meal for tonight." Ally nodded, still feeling upset but knowing that it was only because this moment was so important to her. Helen opened the door and glanced through the crack to see where everybody was. "Coast is clear," she said and she and Ally stepped out. They listened to Jane and

Ally's mum's footsteps coming down the stairs and Helen went back to unpacking the shopping bags.

Ally mustered up a smile as Jane appeared.

"Come on you. Let me give you a tour of outside," she said excitedly.

"Oh, but what about the tea?" Ally's mum said protectively.

"I could really use a hand with tonight's dinner," interrupted Helen, looking dramatically at the clock and then at Ally's mum.

"Oh, very well then. You take Jane outside. I am needed here," Ally's mum said, and with a toss of her hair, she turned towards the kitchen.

Jane raised her eyebrows and made a break for the front door, quickly followed by Ally. Jane paused by the blossom tree. "Hmm, you always said that your blossom tree would stand tall, to mark the place you would call home."

Ally blushed. "I had forgotten about that." She giggled as she hooked her arm through Jane's.

"Let me show you the barn." They began to make their way around the line of trees but were greeted by a group of people. "Is everything alright?" asked Ally. The people all turned their heads in unison and looked at Ally.

Hugh leapt forwards "Yes, of course, Mom. Why wouldn't it be?" asked Hugh, putting on his best puppy look.

"Hmm, now I'm suspicious," said Ally warily. "Anyway, I was just going to show Jane the barn.

"No, you can't!" cried Molly and she jumped forwards to stand next to Hugh.

"Why possibly not?" queried Ally as her body started to stiffen.

Ben caught Jane's eye and motioned with his head towards the trailer. "Umm, because we are in the middle of fixing it, and finishing off your job list," Hugh explained awkwardly. "Come on, Mom. You're just delaying us, just like Grandma does. Let us get on with it. Trust us." He knew his words would hurt as he watched his mum take a step back and her shoulders slump.

"It's been a long trip and there is so much for us to catch up on," said Jane. "How about we hide away in the trailer with a cup of tea," she added naughtily, not quite understanding the secrecy but wanting to be part of it anyway.

"Fantastic. I will bring two teas over to the trailer," offered Molly, rolling up onto her tip toes, ready to sprint. "Don't forget the biscuits," called Jane over her shoulder.

Ally glanced back at Bill, who gave her a nod of reassurance, as she and Jane slipped inside the trailer. "What is that lot up to?" Ally questioned as her mind began to shuffle through a multitude of options, like she was playing a game of chess.

"Who knows," shrugged Jane. "But, if it means

room service, then I am all for it!" She settled into the trailer seats and made herself quite at home and Ally sat down too. Just then, the door opened and Molly's head popped through. She carefully balanced a tray as she made her way up the steps. "There you go," she said as she caught a look of concern on Ally's face. "Don't look so worried. Everything is under control," grinned Molly.

"That's exactly why I am worried," Ally stated, taking hold of the cup.

"You two stay in here for as long as you like, and call if you need more tea," Molly offered, winking at Jane.

Molly ran back to the barn to find Hugh and Aden inside, giving Wildfire a leg stretch. "Phew! That was a close call," she said, sitting down on the hay bales next to them.

"Well, that's the last job on the list," John said gleefully. "Time to start the party." He rubbed his hands together.

"Then I recommend that we bring some of that wood around to the fire pit and grab a beer whilst dinner is being finished," Ben suggested as his happy butterflies began to flutter with anticipation in his chest. He allowed himself a moment to dream of the day that awaited them. "You three still OK to do the horses this evening?" Ben asked.

"Yes, of course," acknowledged Hugh.

As the adults stepped outside the barn, they could feel that the coolness of the evening was beginning to creep in. Ben and Billy grabbed a few handfuls of logs and walked around to the back of the house. John and Sally went inside to gather the drinks.

There was a knock on the trailer door. "Come in," called Ally, giving her and Jane chance to catch their breath from their continuous conversation. "Just wanted to let you know that we will be around by the fire pit whilst we wait for dinner," Bill said warmly.

Ally nodded. "We will be there soon," she replied. Bill smirked. "I know that kind of soon," he said cheekily. "Don't think I don't know what happens when you women get together. There is no such thing as time. So, all I will say is, no rush," he added as he closed the door. Ally and Jane could hear him chuckling to himself as he walked across to the fire pit.

John and Sally stepped out onto the back porch and paused to admire the table. It was set with plates, candles, glasses and fresh flowers. And the aroma of delicious food swirled all around them. "How magical," Sally whispered. John kissed her on her cheek. "Love is magical. I love you," he said as he felt the atmosphere remind him of their love. Sally blushed. "You big softie. Come on. Let's get cosy by the fire," she said, kissing him as she slipped past him. Ben arrived to light the fire and everyone found their place on the benches surrounding the stone pit. Sally and John passed out the drinks and Bill let out a groan as he lowered his body onto the bench. "Ah, that's better," he said as Billy came and sat down next to him. Tom and Chad took the next bench and their usual banter began with Ben. Conversation easily drifted to old stories and before long, the valley filled with the sound of their laughter.

Hugh, Molly and Aden appeared a little later. As they stepped outside the barn, they were greeted by a clear night sky, filled with a blanket of stars. They glanced across and saw that the trailer light was still on. "Mom must still be talking to Jane," Hugh observed. But he was suddenly distracted by the aroma of food. "Wow! What is that smell?" he asked as he walked in the direction of where it was coming from. Molly and Aden happily followed and they all stepped into the house. "That smells amazing," declared Hugh as the warmth from the cooker wafted across his face.

"Hopefully it will taste just as amazing," Helen said, her cheeks rosy from the heat of the oven. "Could you get everyone to the table?" she asked.

"I think we are about ready."

"Yes, most definitely!" offered Hugh as his stomach rumbled with anticipation.

"Where's Ally?" called Ally's mum.

"In the trailer, with Jane," Hugh replied before disappearing outside onto the back porch.

"I will go and get her," stated Ally's mum as she took off her apron. Helen gave her an encouraging smile. Ally's mum paraded across to the trailer but her heart was pounding and her mouth became dry. Her footsteps got heavier as she got closer to the trailer door. She thumped loudly and Jane swung it open. "Oh," Ally's mum said, a little surprised. "Dinner is ready and getting cold," she added bluntly.

"Well then, we best go across before it all disappears," replied Jane, trying to warm the moment.

"That would be a good idea," coughed Ally's mum. "I just need a word with Ally first though." Jane glanced back worriedly at Ally, but Ally motioned that it was OK for her to go. Jane stepped cautiously outside as Ally's mum stepped inside and closed the door, leaving Jane standing there in the darkness.

"Would you like to sit down?" Ally asked politely.

"No," replied her mum frankly.

Ally folder her arms across her chest. "So, you wanted to talk?" she queried, reflecting her mum's cold tone of voice, but her palms were sweaty with nerves.

"Yes," agreed her mum. "Let's just straighten a few things out before tomorrow. I know what you have all been saying about me. Don't think the wind doesn't carry your harsh words," she spat out as a fire burned in her belly.

"I only said those things because they are true," Ally shot back as she stood up and took the bait.

"Well maybe one day you will understand why I am doing this the way that I am. It's about time your feet were placed firmly back on the ground," snarled Ally's mum in retaliation.

"What on earth are you talking about?" questioned Ally. "My feet are on the ground. It's just that my life is no longer a horror story, but is actually turning out to be OK," she said, slapping her hands on her sides in frustration. "Why do you want me to be miserable for the rest of my life?" She was exhausted from the words that had already wounded her.

"I don't want you to be miserable! I am your mother. That's the last thing I want you to be. I just don't want history to repeat itself and for you have to go through it all again!" screamed Ally's mum.

Ally paused as the truth was finally revealed. "You

are afraid of me loosing Ben?" she said quietly as it all began to make sense and her thoughts called out 'check mate'.

"I have had to pick you up off that kitchen floor so many times," said her mum wearily. "I don't want to have to do it all again." Her anger subsided and tears began to well up in her eyes.

Ally took hold of her mum's shoulders. "That will never happen again!" she stated firmly. "At some point, decades from now, yes, Ben will go as well. But, I will never go back to that place of darkness again. Nor will I spend the rest of my life running from it, or letting it dictate my choices because I'm afraid of it returning. I am OK, and I will always be OK," she said, looking deeply into her mum's eyes. "It's all going to be OK."

Ally felt her mum's body begin to melt between her fingers. "How do you know?" asked her mum, with her head bowed.

"I don't," replied Ally simply. "I just have to believe it won't happen again. But if it does, I know now how to turn things around. I have to trust myself," Ally explained, wrapping her mum in a hug. She felt her mum take a large breath in and sigh deeply. "But to go around micromanaging everything to try and avoid things happening that are out of our control anyway, will only cause more problems. And it means that we will miss out on receiving the gifts that life wants to give to us." Ally took in a breath. "I don't need a sergeant major to boss me around and tell me how to avoid tripping over my own mistakes. I need a mum who will brush off my grazes and wrap me in a hug and let me know that everything is OK. A mum who will get me back on my feet and give me an encouraging nudge to try again."

Ally's mum stepped back and wiped her tear-stained cheeks. "OK," she sniffed. "I will try." She felt such relief wash over her as the burden she had been carrying fell to the ground.
"That's all I ask," Ally said empathetically. "Come on. We best get to that dinner table before Bill eats the lot!" Ally laughed, lightening the mood. They both walked out of the trailer and across to the house, hand in hand, heart to heart.
"I am just going to tidy myself up a bit," said Ally's mum. "I can't have everybody seeing me like this." She walked across the living room and headed up the stairs.
Helen opened the back door. "All sorted?" she questioned hopefully.
Ally nodded. "All sorted." She stepped outside to see the table surrounded by all those she loved and held most dearly. All those who had been a stepping stone along her journey to this point. As she took a seat next to Ben, he handed her a glass of champagne. "Here's to life's greatest

gifts," John announced. Ally's mum slipped outside and took a seat next to Helen. She took hold of a glass too. "Cheers!" chorused everybody and the clinking of glasses echoed around the table.

"Let's eat!" cried Hugh, delving into the stew pot. "Yes!" he screamed with excitement. "I thought there could be no better meal than the one we had before you met Ben," Helen said, pleased with herself.
"Thank you," Ally whispered as her hands touched her heart and her eyes glistened with gratitude. The smell transported her back to that very moment.

6 THE BIG DAY

Molly lay by Ally's side and gently played with her hair. She watched each strand cascade softly through her fingertips. Molly was deep in thought as she realised just how quickly her life had changed. What seemed like forever at the time, was actually only a tiny drop in her life. She blinked and brought her attention back to the room. Ally was staring at her. "That was quite a conversation you were having in there," Ally observed, gently tapping Molly's head.

Molly blushed. "I was just thinking," she whispered.

"About your mum and dad?" Ally asked sympathetically.

Molly shook her head. "No, about how far we have come. About how many experiences we have had - the bad and the ugly - all leading us up to this moment of celebration. Sometimes I forget that life gives more than it takes away. I get so tied up with what has gone on that I can't always see what I have gained each day," she said as another piece of Ally's hair fell to the pillow. "Very wise, Molly. You are a clone of your Nana," Ally said as she sat herself upright in bed.

There was a tap on the door. "Can we come in?" a gentle voice said from outside. "Yes, of course," replied Ally, staring down at her cow-print pyjamas and beginning to regret her choice. Helen, Jane, Sally and Ally's mum all filtered in and perched on the bed. Jane handed Ally her morning cup of tea. "Any sign of the men?" Ally asked taking the cup gratefully from Jane.

"Don't you worry about them," Jane replied. "They are under strict orders."

"Are you ready for your gift?" Sally asked with a mischievous look in her eye.

"Gift?" questioned Ally. "You shouldn't have. You all being here is the best gift I could have asked for."

"Now, now," interjected Ally's mum. "Listen to your own words. Don't get in the way of life giving you a gift. Instead, open yourself up to receive. Just say 'thank you' rather than 'no'."

"OK, lead on," said Ally, motioning with her arm. "They all got up and made their way out onto the landing. Ally peered over the balcony, and there, hung on the wall of the stairway, was a string of lights. And under each light, was a photograph.

"Wow!" breathed Ally. She made her way over to the photographs, and as she moved along the line, she touched each one tenderly. Every photograph captured a moment in time, a segment of their journey, their dreams and who they were becoming. "This is incredible," Ally whispered in amazement. She carefully scanned the black and white photos of Billy and Nana O, standing together. And of the house back when Ben's grandad bought it. Ally could no longer contain her tears. "The greatest gift of all," she sobbed. "The gift of time."

Ally was speechless, and the women all smiled at the success of their gift. "Now, come on. There is a lot to do," stated Ally's mum, clapping her hands together and pulling everyone out of their trance. Ally peeled herself away from the wall and made her way back upstairs. "You go and have your shower whilst we organise breakfast," offered Helen. Ally made her way back to her room but her legs felt unsteady as she began to realise that the day she had dreamed of was coming true. She listened to the drumming of feet as everybody went down into the kitchen, and the hum of excitement that floated in the air.

"I have written out the day's itinerary," stated Ally's mum, placing a piece of paper on the kitchen table.

"Now I know where Ally gets it from," laughed Sally.

"The hairdresser should be here any minute," continued Ally's mum, seemingly oblivious to the joke. "So, if Jane and Sally, you go first. Helen and I will finish preparing the food. Then it's Molly and Ally's turn."

Ally appeared at the kitchen doorway. "What are you all planning now?" she asked, taking a seat at the kitchen table.

"Never you mind. You just relax," said her mum, slipping the piece of paper under the table and onto her lap.

"Right then, here are the bacon sandwiches," announced Helen as she placed them in the centre of the table with a big pot of tea. But they all paused as they heard the front door creak open. They turned their heads to find Bill peeking his head around the doorframe. He drew in a long breath through his nostrils. "Mmm...is there a spare sandwich going for me?" he asked cheekily.

"Get out you naughty goat!" Helen said, throwing a kitchen towel towards him. Bill quickly ducked back outside and scampered across to the trailers. Just then, the front door began to re-open again and Helen got her next weapon of choice ready. A head peered around and Helen got into position. But it was an unfamiliar woman. "Is it

alright to come in?" she asked tentatively.
Helen quickly lowered her weapon. "Yes, of
course! You must be the hairdresser. Come in,
come in. You can set yourself up in the living
room," she said warmly.
Ally's mum leapt to her feet with excitement.
"Jane, Sally, come on, you're first. No time to
loiter."

Molly slipped away from the kitchen table
and disappeared quietly upstairs to her bedroom.
She walked over to her chest of drawers and
gently pulled out the bottom drawer. She peeled
back a layer of clothes and took out the engraved
owl box from Nana O. She carefully opened the lid
and lifted out the letter that Nana O had written
to her. Molly ran her fingers over the writing. "I
wish you were here today, Nana O. You would be
making us all laugh." She wrapped her fingers
tightly around the box, to absorb the strength she
was looking for to make it through the day.
Just then, Ally cautiously opened the door. "May I
come in?" she asked. Molly quickly put the letter
back in the box, placed it in the drawer and
pushed it closed.

Ally entered, perched on the bed and Molly
came and joined her. "I can't wait to see you in
your dress," smiled Ally. They both glanced up at
Molly's bridesmaid's dress, hanging on her

wardrobe door. It was a soft, yellow dress with a silk bow on the corner. The material gathered underneath the bow and cascaded down, like a waterfall. The bow sparkled in the morning sunlight. Molly smiled. "But, there is something missing," Ally stated teasingly. "It's not quite complete." And she placed a box in Molly's lap. "That should do it," smiled Ally with pure delight. Molly gently opened the box and lifted out a charm bracelet. "Ally! It's so beautiful," cried Molly, and she flung her arms around Ally's neck. "Thank you," she whispered.

Ally pointed to each charm. "There is a robin for your Nana O, two stars for your parents, the house is me and Ben, the map is Hugh and then, of course, the horse is for Red Rock and Firefly. You can keep adding to it as you make your way through life. It's there to remind you of all those you have around you who love you so dearly. No matter where you are, this will always be your home and we will always be your family."
Molly began to cry with joy. "I don't know what to say," she sobbed.
"Some moments don't need words," Ally said, kissing her on the forehead.

"Molly!" called Ally's mum. "Are you ready? It's your turn next. Come down to the living room." They playfully rolled their eyes at each other.

Molly held out her arm and Ally gently clipped the charm bracelet in place before Molly answered her call. Ally paused a moment and glanced up at the dress once more. Another wave of gratitude washed over her and her eyes began to well up. "I need more tea," she sniffed, blinking away the feeling. She got up and made her way back downstairs. She could hear the clattering of pans in the kitchen and the constant conversation in the living room. She saw numerous shadows moving around outside. It was a whirlwind of chaotic love, putting the final touches to a single moment awaiting to be lived. "Anyone else for a fresh cup of tea?" Ally asked and she was met with a chorus of 'yes's'. She lined the cups up on the worktop, before quickly disappearing into the office to get the flowers for her hair. But she paused as she caught sight of the three, framed pieces of paper above the desk. She gently blew a kiss to the frame in the centre. It was her and Ben's dreams that they had written together, simply entitled: *Our Dream*.

On her return, she found Jane in the midst of finishing off the teas. "Your turn, Ally," said Molly, getting out of the chair. Her hair was now mostly pinned up, with just a few curls, hanging loosely around her face. Ally felt another wave of gratitude for the young woman that Molly was becoming. "You look beautiful," Ally said with pride.

Jane placed a warm cup in Ally's hand. "You'll be needing this," she said as she guided Ally into the chair. Ally felt the magical fingertips of the hairdresser as she began the transformation. Ally gently handed the yellow roses and peace lilies to the hairdresser, who expertly intertwined them into Ally's hair. The hairdresser continued to make easy conversation but Ally remained silent as she absorbed this special moment. She tuned into Jane and Sally's laughter, the chinking of Molly's charm bracelet and the orders being bounced around the kitchen.

"There we go. What do you think?" asked the hairdresser as she took a step back to inspect her work. Everyone fell silent and their jaws dropped open.

"No time for catching flies," instructed Ally's mum. "Go and get your dresses on. We are 3 minutes behind schedule!" She clapped her hands together again, interrupting the moment. Jane looked at Ally and rolled her eyes, but they all proceeded upstairs to get into their outfits. Only Helen remained and she now sat down in the chair, ready for her transformation to begin.

Ally stepped into her room and closed the door behind her. She could hear Sally and Jane helping each other into their dresses, and Molly gently humming as she stepped into hers too.

And then the gasps from Jane and Sally as they all admired each other. Today, it felt like they were all shining from the happiness. Ally reached under the bed and pulled out her dress box. She gently lifted the lid to reveal the dress that she had picked up. As she lifted it out, her gaze drifted over the crystals, intertwined with the lace and silk, and glistening in the sunshine. Ally slipped off her pyjamas and stepped into her dress. She slowly did up the buttons and tied the ribbon around her waist. She glanced at herself in the mirror, hardly recognising the woman staring back at her.

Soft lace lay across Ally's shoulders and down her arms. The body of the dress was made of silk but with a gentle overlay of lace. The skirt floated around her and hundreds of sparkles glistened in the light. A yellow ribbon lay around her waist, with a bow to the side, and the tassels draped down her side, to the floor. Ally slipped on some plain, white shoes and hung the locket that Ben had given her around her neck. "Well, I never would have imagined that this was the woman I would become," Ally said to her reflection as she turned from side to side. "Life sure does have a strange way of sorting everything out." She ran her fingers down the dress to smooth out some imaginary creases. She paused and felt, for the first time, that she was the woman she had been yearning to become.

Ally took one final look as she swirled around and around. The skirt lifted and floated in the air, and the sparkles glistened in the sunlight that beamed through the bedroom window. She was ready. She headed out along the landing, and listened to the rest of the women getting ready. Ally tiptoed along, glancing in the mirror of miracles that still hung between Hugh and Molly's bedrooms, and snuck downstairs. As she stood in the centre of the living room with her dress sparkling and her cheeks glowing, she felt a peace like never before. A noise at the top of the stairs broke her trance and she glanced up to see Molly standing there. Molly's jaw dropped open. "Quick, everyone! Ally is ready!" she yelled. There was an eruption of thundering feet and then five heads peered over the banister. There was then silence as they all slowly made their way downstairs, not once taking their eyes off Ally.

It was Jane who eventually broke the silence as they all stood in front of Ally. "I hope you brought plenty of tissues! You tinker. You're already ruining my make-up," Jane said in jest as she tried to wipe away her tears of joy without smudging her mascara. "May I come in," called a voice from the front door as Bill started to enter. "Well, don't you look like mother nature's finest

creation?" Bill said, openly admiring Ally.
"Alright, alright! That's enough attention," Ally said, shuffling uncomfortably and starting to blush.
Bill stepped forwards. "It has only just begun, my dear. Are we all ready?" he asked. "Because we are ready for you outside."

"Yes, we are all set," said Ally's mum as she stood next to Helen. Jane moved to stand next to Sally, and Molly took her place behind them. Bill held out his arm and Ally linked hers with his. The relief, that he was there by her side, washed over her and her legs became like jelly.
"Let's go then," Bill suggested and Helen and Ally's mum stepped out the front door first, and down the porch steps. Sally and Jane followed as the sunlight streamed through the door. Molly took one final glance behind, and Ally gave her a smile of reassurance, before she too headed out. Ally felt Bill give her arm a squeeze as they began to step towards the door. With every step she took, she felt the anticipation grow and her grip tighten.

Ally's eyes grew wider with apprehension and she gulped in another bubble of air. She walked out onto the front porch and heard the movement of numerous bodies standing up. She hadn't even noticed the other guests arriving that morning.

She blinked against the bright sunlight, trying to focus her eyes. As they adjusted, the only image that became clear was the man in the grey suit, standing next to the blossom tree. His hands were placed gently in front of him and he had a smile on his face which was growing by the second. All the rest was a blur. She suddenly felt a gentle pull on her arm. She hadn't realised that she had stopped walking.

Ally remained focused on the man standing in front of her. She fixed her eyes on Ben and took each step carefully, making sure not to trip. Ben's eyes glistened and he didn't hold back the rush of unconditional love that he felt for the person walking towards him. He held out his hand and Ally reached gratefully for it. She sighed with relief as she felt the warmth of his touch travel up her arm and around her body. She was home.

Ally and Ben stood facing each other, hand in hand, in front of the blossom tree. The rows of seats were filled with all those they held most dear to their hearts. Everybody was ready to witness the commitment that was about to be made. The vicar stepped forwards. "Are we ready to begin?" he asked. Ally and Ben nodded gently. Ally could hear the vicar's voice but his words dripped off her as she stared deeply into Ben's eyes. She felt wave after wave of unconditional love radiate off them both. He gently stroked her fingers with his, and the sunlight danced off the sparkles on her dress like a thousand shooting stars. Ben couldn't contain his smile. "Ben, if you wouldn't mind?" said the vicar, momentarily breaking his gaze. Ben blushed before carefully picking a ring off a branch on the blossom tree. He slipped it on Ally's finger. Ally took the other ring off the same branch and placed it tenderly on Ben's finger. "I now pronounce you, with so much delight, husband and wife," smiled the vicar.

Ben immediately stepped forwards, wrapped his arms around Ally's waist and kissed her lips with such tender care and love. He stuttered to find his words. He simply couldn't stop smiling for long enough to form a sentence. So, he surrendered and decided to pick Ally up instead and twirl her around – just like the first night they had met. They were serenaded by cheers from all of the guests and Ally's laughter echoed around the driveway. Ben's smile grew even bigger. He reluctantly lowered her back to the ground but intertwined his hand with hers. He wanted to hold onto their love and the future, but most importantly, each other's hearts.

They started to walk down the centre aisle

which had been created by the guests, who threw yellow and white rose petals over them both. Molly, awash with happiness, let the tears gleefully roll down her cheeks as she threw yet another handful of rose petals. She felt Hugh step behind her and wrap his arms around her shoulders. "Hey, you two. Look," Aden said, pointing at the blossom tree. There, sat on the top branch watching over it all, was a robin. "You don't think...?" queried Molly.

"Ha-ha. You don't think your Nana O would miss out on a party like this, do you?" Billy asked as he moved to stand next to them. "She will take whatever form she needs in order to answer who has called upon her. That robin has been sitting there the whole time. And I am sure, will continue to visit us," Billy added, patting Molly on the shoulder. He then turned to follow the throng of guests, who were now heading towards the back of the house.

Molly stepped towards the blossom tree and looked up at the robin. "I knew you would answer me. Thank you, Nana O," Molly whispered as she gently touched the locket and then her new bracelet. She turned and happily skipped along to join the rest of the guests.

"Hugh, can I have a quick word?" Ben said as he tried to navigate his way through all the 'congratulations' from people. He motioned towards the back door of the house. They both made their way inside the living room, the one place that seemed to have held onto its tranquillity and silence. "Just give me a second," Ben said as he darted into the office. Hugh fidgeted and glanced outside. He was eager to get back to the party. He turned back around to find Ben standing there, who motioned for Hugh to sit down on the sofa.

"Oh, but...," groaned Hugh, pointing towards the guests.

"It will only take a minute," Ben reassured him as he sat down and patted the seat next to him.

Hugh grudgingly walked across and plonked himself down, next to Ben. Ben cleared his throat. "I wanted to give you this. Not only to say thank you for making this day the best day of my life. But also to remind you that some dreams aren't meant to be forgotten." Ben handed Hugh a brown box.

Hugh opened the lid but looked confused. "But this is your...," he stammered. "You love this."

"I have a new belt now," explained Ben. "One that I am going to wear with pride. It's the prize of my family," said Ben as he tilted his buckle to show Hugh.

"I don't know what to say," cried Hugh. "Thank you," he stuttered as he hurled his arms around

Ben.

"I know that one day, you will get your own one of these, but just always remember, you are my champion!" Ben said, kissing him on top of his head and squeezing him in a hug.

Hugh slipped off his black belt and threaded his new one through his belt loops. He looked up at Ben and beamed with confidence. "Now you can go back and join the party," Ben said with a wink, and Hugh sprinted out the door. Ben watched Hugh dart towards Molly and Aden, and show them his new belt. Ben paused a moment as he began to reflect on what his home and life had transformed into. All those tough decisions and growing pains were definitely worth it. His attention was suddenly caught by Ally who was making her way across the back porch and in through the door. "Hey, Mr," she said delicately. "Hey, Mrs," he replied as he watched Ally glide towards the kitchen, in all her elegance and radiance. Her beauty took his breath away. "I am so incredibly lucky," he whispered to himself as he looked up to the ceiling.

Ben stood as he heard the kettle being filled. "Thirsty work," he said, getting a cup out of the cupboard for Ally.
Ally draped her arms around Ben's waist and gently rested her head on his chest. "That's

better," she muttered.

Ben softly ran his hands up and down her arms. "You look stunning!" Ben began. "Not just today. But every day. When you dress up or when your dress down, you are so beautiful to me. I have never met a woman like you. We just fit together in ways I never knew were possible. You have changed me for the better and I can't wait to continue along this journey, with you by my side. Because, whatever we have to face, I know we will make it through."

Ally squeezed Ben more tightly. She looked up and kissed him on the lips. "The day I met you was the greatest day of my life. But today is definitely hot second," chuckled Ally as she continued to make her cup of tea.

Ben and Ally made their way back outside. As they stepped out onto the back porch, the guests cheered again and raised their glasses. "To the new Mr & Mrs!" John shouted out.

"To the new Mr & Mrs!" the guests all chorused back in unison. Ben pulled Ally in close. She precariously balanced her cup of tea, trying not to christen her dress with the first stain of the day quite so soon. "Come on! Let's go and celebrate," Ben said as they walked down the steps and became lost, once more, in the crowd. Ally watched her friends topping up the guest's glasses, and Helen began to line the table with glorious foods. The sun illuminated the day, and the countryside created a backdrop for the most perfect picture of them all.

"You have done a fantastic job," Bill said as he crept up behind Helen. She was just putting the rest of the food out onto the table.
"Well, I am trusting you to taste-test it all, and report back," she responded cheekily.
"I'll take one for the team and do my best, even if it means I have to go up a clothes size," Bill said, standing up tall, puffing his chest out and sucking in his stomach.
Helen burst into laughter. "I knew I could count on you."

Ben watched Ally meander around, catching up with old acquaintances and meeting new faces. He couldn't keep his eyes off her. Ally glanced across, made eye contact and beamed a smile of joy back to him.
"Well then, that's all our fun and partying over with," said Tom, slapping Ben on the back and breaking the moment.
Ben glanced at him. "The partying ended years ago. You just haven't realised it," he replied.
"Well, as long as she doesn't distract you too much," mock-warned Tom. "Otherwise I'll be having words," he added playfully. He turned to walk away, but abruptly stopped. "However, if she

keeps cooking those fantastic dinners, then I will just have to come over a lot more for training," he said, pointing his finger in the air.

The exhilarating atmosphere continued to grow as the guests sat eating, or mingling with each other. As they caught up with new and old friends, stories floated in the air from past and present. In time, the sun began to set, creating an explosive display of different colours in the sky. Even the clouds seemed to dance as they drifted by. Billy grabbed a drink, lit the fire pit and sat to watch the setting sun. "May I join you?" said a voice behind him. He turned to find Ally's mum standing there.
"Of course," said Billy and he slid across to make room for her. He glanced awkwardly at her, unsure of who was going to start the conversation.
"Thank you for embracing Ally so warmly into your family," Ally's mum said, not taking her eyes off the ever-changing colours of the sunset sky.

"Your Ally has helped me more than I could ever possibly help her," said Billy sincerely. "She gave me back my son. And made two stubborn mules forgive each other. Not something that's easily achieved," he explained, taking a sip of his drink.
Ally's mum nodded. "Family, hey? Complicated

things, and you never seem to feel like you're getting it quite right. You always seem to be wondering what would have happened if you had done things differently. And then one day, you realise that they are all grown up, and that they turned out OK, despite you," she sighed, with a smile.

"That sounds about right," agreed Billy.

"You all seem to have set up a great life here," said Ally's mum. "And a very bright future is ahead of Molly and Hugh. I have never seen them so happy."

"Well, sometimes I think you outgrow your past, but perhaps don't realise it until you move on and start to receive your new dreams," Billy added. Ally's mum just nodded in agreement. "Hugh and Molly, I am sure, are going to bring plenty of interesting twists and turns to our road ahead. I don't think we can retire from family life just yet."

Billy laughed and Ally's mum began to laugh with him. "No, you're quite right," she chuckled. They fell into comfortable silence as they watched the last slither of sun disappear behind the horizon. The night sky rolled across and, one by one, the stars began to shine.

A sudden clatter behind them caused them to turn around, but it was just the band beginning to set up, ready for the evening ahead. "Can we have your attention please?" said a voice over the microphone. It was the singer in the band. "We would just like to say thank you for letting us be part of your special day, and we hope to see the dancefloor full until the early hours.

"Don't worry! I have my comfy shoes on. I am ready!" shouted Jane across the garden, causing everyone to laugh.

"Young lady, you're on!" replied the singer as his fingers ran over the strings of his guitar, and the violinist pulled back his bow. "OK, if you would all like to make your way onto the dancefloor, aka the patch of grass in front of me, we shall start off as we mean to go on!"

Everyone put down their plates and walked over to the band. Hugh and Molly positioned themselves right at the front. "Are you ready, Hugh?" asked the singer. Hugh gave a big thumbs up but then ran across to Ally.

"Sorry, Ben. But I am going to have the first dance," he said mischievously. "Ready!" Hugh shouted back to the singer.

Just then, Molly ran across to Ben. "Can I dance with you?" she asked sweetly.

"I would be honoured," Ben said as he bowed. The band started to play, the music radiated out of the speakers, and realisation dawned across Ally's face.

"Life is a highway! I wanna ride it all night long," sang Hugh at the top of his lungs, as he swung Ally from side to side. They wiggled their hips, waved their arms, and Ben and Molly jiggled their way across to link hands with them. They all continued to sing along, at the tops of their voices - the rest of the guests too – and the singer was soon drowned out by the noise of his new congregation.

The dance floor continued to thrive as Bill twirled Helen around, Billy danced with Jane, and Sally, John and Aden bounced and bobbed along to the music. They atmosphere became electric with joy, love flowed abundantly and everyone's concerns melted into the ground. In this moment, they were all free.

'BANG!' Everyone stopped, including the singer. "What was that?" Ally asked with concern in her voice.
"I am not sure," said Ben. "I will go and take a look." His shoulders stiffened protectively.
Another noise came from around the front of the house. "That sounds like a loose horse," Ally cried, breaking out into a run. Everyone followed. As she reached the other side of the house, her dress hemmed in dirt, she stopped. "What the cupcake is this?" she exclaimed. Her gaze descended on the bum of a brown and white

horse, which was sticking out of the front door. There soon followed a screech. "Get off the porch, you furry thing! Get out!" cried Ally's mum as she tried to shoo the horse away. The horse edged backwards onto the front porch and stared at everyone, with cake icing around its lips. "Ben," said Ally, feigning anger. "Do you have something you need to tell me?" She folded her arms across her chest.

Ben sheepishly weaved through the throng of guests towards Ally. "A present for you," he declared. He painted a smile on his face but couldn't quite tell if Ally's reaction was good or not.

"Go on! Horses don't live in houses," Ally's mum continued, wafting a towel towards it. Ally couldn't contain herself anymore and she broke into a fit of laughter.

Billy handed Ben a halter and Ben hurriedly ran to secure it around the horse's head. "Meet Wildfire," he said as he laid his hand on Wildfire's back.

Ally gently walked up to Wildfire and ran her hand along his neck. She couldn't help but leak a smile. "So this means that I'll be getting back in the saddle then?" she asked, raising her eyebrows.

Ben shuffled his feet awkwardly. "Well, it's just an idea," he murmured.

Ally kissed him on the cheek. "I love it," she declared. "But maybe not in this dress!"

Ben let out a sigh of relief. "I'll just go and...," he said as he nodded towards the barn. Ally nodded her agreement. There was a noise then from around the other side of the house, as the band began to play once more. "Come on! Let's get back to that dance floor," Hugh suggested as he ushered the guests back around.

Ally looked at the frustration in her mum's face. "It's ruined!" stated her mum. "That four-legged, pooing machine has ruined it."

Ally stepped through and saw that the cake now had a large horse's nose dent in it. Her hand quickly flung to her face as she tried to smother her giggles. "It's not totally ruined," she chuckled. "If you look at it from this angle, it looks perfectly fine." Ally's mum responded with a disapproving frown.

"Don't panic," said Helen. "I have just the thing." She came to the rescue and placed three yellow roses neatly inside the dent. "There, now people will think that it was meant to be there." She stood back to admire her solution. "To be honest though, with Bill around, I give that cake 5 minutes before he makes his own dent in it!" They all began to laugh as Helen and Ally's mum picked it up and took it outside. Ally looked longingly at the sofa. Oh, what she wouldn't give just to slip on her pyjamas and put on a movie.

Ben read her thoughts. "Not a chance," he said with a smirk. "We have more dancing to do." Ally felt the warmth of his hand on her back as he escorted her out the door and back to the party. As they stood at the top of the steps, Ben signalled to the band to pause a moment. "If we could just have your attention please," Ben shouted, clearing his throat. Everyone quietened and turned to face Ben and Ally. "We would just like to take this opportunity to thank you all for coming today, and making this one of the best days of our lives. To those of you who helped put this day together, you are saints. We couldn't have pulled it off without you. But most of all, I would like to take this opportunity to say, to this incredible woman, that I can't wait to watch the sun rise and set each day, with you by my side. And to watch Hugh and Molly grow and develop, and teach us a new perspective on life that only their innocence can see. I can't wait to hold your heart in my hands, and to continue to be reminded of the country man I am. I'll try to be the best version of myself that I can be, for you, each day. I love you, Miss Ally, and may I be your last everything."

Ally wiped away a tear and smiled. "Well,

what can I say to that?" she asked. "You have all made this day so magical, a true fairy tale for me and my family. Not only can I rejoice in the ring I now wear in honour of the unconditional love I will eternally have for this man. But also in our family, which has been bonded with this love as well. To the friends who I see as my family, you have turned our dream into this beautiful moment, and one that I shall never forget. And as for you," Ally said, turning to Ben. "You brought me back to life, and showed me what it means to be loved. You have helped me remember the woman I was meant to be. And I hope that every day brings opportunities for my love to shine. You are patient with me, yet you will stand shoulder to shoulder with me when I need strength. I can't wait to lay my head next to yours each night. Not only are you life's greatest gift to me, but I open my heart fully to receive that gift each day. Through trials and triumphs, my hand and heart will always be with yours."

An echo of clapping exploded from everyone as Ben and Ally kissed. Hugh and Molly ran up to them both and they all hugged. "I love you, monkeys," Ally said, bending down and kissing them both on top of their heads. "Now, let's go and dance," she said with glee. The band started up again and everyone filtered back to the dancefloor, wearing a huge smile.

7 THE GREATEST GIFT, THE GIFT OF TIME

"My goodness," groaned Jane. "The salesperson said these were the comfiest shoes you could buy." She sat at the kitchen table rubbing an aching foot. She let out another groan at the relief she felt once she had finally freed both her feet.

Sally laughed. "Well, I must admit, I haven't seen anyone dance quite as vigorously as you do."

Jane let out another groan.

"Jane has always been the first on the dancefloor, and the last one to leave," Ally said as she entered the kitchen. "Hugh, Aden and Molly fell straight to sleep as soon as their heads hit the pillow," Ally smiled. "They have created a super-bed on Hugh's floor, using all the duvets and cushions," she added as she perched on Ben's knee.

"Well, I think that all went pretty well, don't you?" John said, stretching back in his chair and placing his hands behind his head.

"I would raise a glass to that," Ben agreed.

"Right. Night, all," said Helen as she and Bill passed the kitchen.

"I need to go and sleep off some of this food," Bill added with a wink, patting his stomach.

"Thank you again, Helen, for organising all the food. It really was amazing. You should go into business," urged Ally.

"Ha! No thanks. I like being retired," Helen replied with a dismissive wave of her hand. Her and Bill disappeared outside.

"I think I will follow on," yawned Billy, placing his hat on his head. "See you all in the morning."

"Goodnight!" shouted Ally's mum from the stairs.

"And then there were just 7 left standing," observed Tom.

"Well, to be honest," said John. "I think I am going to follow the crowd, as I am sure there will be an Ally-list ready for us in the morning," he teased as he and Sally stood up.

Ally got up and gave them both a hug. "You two are legends, and I look forward to the day that I can repay all that you have done for us."

"Nonsense," dismissed Sally. "We loved every minute." And she gave Ally an extra squeeze.

"Ben, are you up for a card game?" asked Tom with a lucky glint in his eye.
"Not for me, Buddy," Ben said as he pulled Ally further back into his lap.
"Alright then, just me and Chad. Get ready to lose!" Tom declared, banging his hands on the table.
"You're on!" Chad replied. The two men stood and faced each other, nose-to-nose, before marching their way back to the trailer.

"And then there were three," said Jane as she downed her last drops of tea. "Well, I love you both, but there is a comfy bed calling my name. Ouch!" She winced as she stood up on her aching feet.
"When will you learn?" Ally chuckled, shaking her head.
"Never will I ever grow old!" Jane proclaimed as she championed her empty cup in the air. "But it just may take me a little longer to recover." She laughed as she walked towards the front door, making every step she took look excruciatingly painful.

"What about you?" Ally asked, wrapping her arms around Ben's neck.
"Well, I think I am going to take my wife upstairs

and have her fall asleep in my arms," he said as he lifted Ally up, causing her to giggle. He walked precariously towards the stairs, taking one step at a time.

"I can walk you know," argued Ally playfully.

"No. No, I've got this," Ben said as he huffed and puffed, and his face reddened. He finally reached the top of the stairs, but his breathlessness caused Ally to giggle even more. "Shh, you'll wake everyone up," hissed Ben. But his words had the opposite effect on Ally and she had to bury her head in his shoulder to smother her giggles. Ben felt her body shake with laughter. But he managed to make it through the bedroom door. He casually kicked it closed with his foot behind them. The moment finally came to an end.

As dawn broke, Billy sat at his living room table and glanced around the house. Dust particles glinted in the air. In front of him, lay letters and forms from his solicitor. His hand continued to hover over the dotted line, as he internally debated whether or not this was the correct time. "Please, someone. Give me some guidance," he demanded quietly. His pen dropped to the table and splashed ink across the page. He ran his hands through his hair, closed his eyes and hung his head.

Just then, there was a tap at the window and

Billy jumped to attention. He looked up to see a small sparrow tapping its beak against the glass. '*Tap, tap, tap*'. Billy looked perplexed. '*Tap, tap, tap*'. Billy slowly got up from his chair so as not to spook the bird, and lowered himself down so that he was in line with the window ledge. '*Tap, tap, tap*', continued the sparrow. "Alright, I get the message," Billy acknowledged. The sparrow tapped once more and then flew promptly away to sit on Billy's log pile.

Billy got to his feet and shook his head. He walked over to his bookshelf and pulled out an old, tatty, leather book. "I wonder if it's in here," he muttered as he flicked through the pages. He suddenly stopped. "Yes, there," he said. '*Sparrow: to work as a community as your heart opens more to the giving and receiving of love*'. Billy snapped the book closed. "Alright then," he said decisively. He leant over the page and his pen whizzed his signature across the dotted line. He bundled it back into the paper envelope, slotted it under his arm, grabbed his hat and headed out to his truck.

He placed the paper envelope on the passenger seat, reversed the truck and then drove rapidly down the driveway to the road. He glanced in his rear view mirror and there, sitting on a branch of the tree, was the sparrow.

"Persistent little bird," he muttered. "Doesn't he trust that I will do it?" he queried as he turned towards the little town. As the countryside became scattered with buildings, Billy swerved into a small carpark and came to a stop outside one of the buildings. He gingerly turned off his engine and put the car into park.

He quickly glanced around. "I bet that sparrow has followed me," he said warily. Once he saw that the coast was clear though, he stepped out of his truck and closed the door. But, as he turned to head towards the building, a sparrow landed on his bonnet. "Oh, for goodness sake," he said, taking his hat off and wafting it towards the bird, who moved just out of reach of his swipe. "Do you want to come in with me as well?" he asked sarcastically, pressing his hat firmly back on his head, and marching towards the door.

He stepped through the door to be greeted by a cheery, "morning, Billy." The man walked up to Billy and held out his hand.
Billy shook it politely. "Morning, Alan."
"Congratulations to Ben and Ally by the way," continued Alan. Billy just nodded and then held out the paper envelope. "Right, you best come in then," and he signalled for Billy to step through a door, into another office. Billy took off his hat and

sat down in the seat by the desk. Alan sat down in his leather chair and slid out the pieces of paper. "All signed then, I see?" he said. "Are you sure about this, Billy?"
"Yes, it's the right time," replied Billy, rolling his hat between his fingers.
Alan raised up his eyebrows. "Well, if you're sure," he said and he began to sign the piece of paper as well.

"Right, I will get this all filed," said Alan, shuffling the pieces of paper together so that they were all neatly bound. "But, in the meantime, you can give this to Ben," said Alan as he walked across to a filing cabinet and pulled out a brown, paper file. He handed it to Billy. Billy flipped it open to find a letter and a map inside. "Thanks for all of your help with this," Billy mumbled nervously.
"No problem at all, old friend," Alan said reassuringly, taking Billy's hand and shaking it again. "I am just glad it all got sorted out."
Billy smiled meekly as his fingers clutched onto the file.

"See you around," said Billy as he let himself out. His gaze went straight to the bonnet as he headed back to his truck, but the sparrow was nowhere to be seen. He climbed in and tossed the file onto the passenger seat. He reversed out and headed back the way he had come. His fingers tapped out a beat on the steering wheel, in time to the music on the radio. He turned at the traffic light and made his way towards the driveway. His tapping got louder and he began to whistle as well. As he turned the truck, he could see the house come into view. "It looks like a ghost town around here," he said to himself as he parked in front of the house and grabbed the file. He stepped out into total silence and glanced around to see if he could spy any signs of life, anywhere. He slammed his truck door, loudly. Nothing.

Billy skipped up the steps and went into the house, where he was met with yet more silence. He walked into the kitchen and touched the back of his hand to the coffee jar. Cold. He glanced up at the clock which already read 11am. "Well, who would have thought it. One party and they are all wiped out for the day." He began to make a fresh pot of coffee in the hope that the smell would awaken Ben.

Billy sat down at the kitchen table and his fingers continued to tap to the song that was now on repeat in his head. The smell of coffee grew and he got up to make himself a fresh cup. He took slow sips, as he patiently watched the clock hands tick by. As the second hand moved around, the smell of coffee grew stronger. "Ten, nine, eight, seven..." he counted. He started to have a wager with himself. "Six, five..." There was a shuffling noise above him and a click of a door. "Four, three..." And now the sound of footsteps on the stairs. "Two and one," just as Ben turned the corner, into the kitchen. Billy smiled to himself and took another swig of coffee.

"Morning," croaked Ben.

"Afternoon," replied Billy mockingly.

"Do you want another coffee?" asked Ben as he poured himself one.

"Yes, go on then please." Billy handing him his now empty cup. Ben lifted the coffee jar and filled it back up. "I picked this up from your mailbox," Billy said, sliding the brown, paper file across the table to Ben.

Ben pulled out a chair and sat down in his usual seat. He flipped open the file. "Do you know what it is?" he asked as his eyes tried to focus on the letters. He slid the letter across and decided to start with the picture-part first.

"Why would there be a map of the ranch?" queried Ben. "And what's this blue line? That's not our boundary?" Ben decided that he should probably read the letter. "This doesn't make any sense." He scratched his head. "I best call Alan." He was about to get up from his chair.

"The map is correct," Billy said, lowering his coffee cup.

"But it's twice the size of the ranch," Ben said as his confusion grew.

"That's the size of the ranch from today," Billy explained as he stared intensely at Ben.

"But how?" Ben glanced back down at the map. "I thought that was Duncan's land?"

Billy took in a long breath. "When you were 6 years old, you were adamant that you were going to have yourself a piece of land, to protect the countryside. A place that the animals could live. You went on and on about it, creating all these different plans on how you were going to sell sweets at school and have a paper round to do it." Billy paused for another sip of coffee.

"Pa, I don't even remember saying that. I was probably just dreaming," Ben added dismissively.

"When do we ever give up on our dreams?" questioned Billy. "Anyway, I sat down with your grandpa and we approached Duncan. We asked to buy the land off him with the proviso that there would come a day when you would have the land. And that it would then be up to you two to decide what happens. Duncan agreed to the terms and has been looking after the land for the last few decades. But now he is getting on, as we all are, and it seemed like the right time for you to find out. Now, Son, you can protect the animals and the countryside, just like you dreamed of as a little boy. But know that this land is also the gift of time. I hope you pass on that lesson," Billy said, slotting his thumbs into his jeans pockets as he leant back in his chair.

Ben's face turned to shock. "Do you know what this means?" Ben said as the realisation dawned on him.

"Yes, I do, Son. You need to get a tracker for those two kids of yours, as they could get lost for days out there on one of their adventures!" Billy laughed. Ben shook his head. "You're right about that."

"What's Billy right about?" asked Ally as she appeared at the kitchen doorway.

"You best sit down, Ally," said Ben.

Ally froze. "No! The last time you said those words, something terrible happened."

"Well, this is something good. I promise," reassured Ben, pulling out a chair for her.

Ally cautiously sat down and Ben slid the file across to her. Ally looked over the map. "I don't get it," she said looking up at Ben.

Ben smiled as his finger traced a line. "This was the boundary of the house yesterday," he explained. "And this is the boundary of the house today," he said, pointing at another line.

"What? How is that possible?" asked Ally in amazement.

Ben looked across at Billy. "Call it a wedding present." Billy shrugged his shoulders.

"We...can't possibly..." stammered Ally. "Yes you can," replied Billy. "I am not doing all that paperwork again." He tapped his fingers firmly on the table.
Ally raised up her hands. "I don't know what to say," she breathed. "It's incredible, it's..." She looked at Ben for help with finding her words.
"It means that we are set for life," Ben said, taking hold of Ally's hand and giving it a squeeze. Ally's hands flew to her mouth in shock. "You mean it's solved?" she whispered. Ben nodded excitedly. Ally got up and ran around the kitchen table to wrap Billy in a hug.
"Alright, alright," Billy said awkwardly, patting Ally on the back. Ally felt Billy become rigid so she backed off slightly to give him space to catch his breath.

Ally stood a moment, shaking her head in utter disbelief. Ben took hold of the brown, paper file and closed it. "I think we should wait until everybody has gone before we tell Molly and Hugh. I know they will want to head straight off to explore it," he said. "And I best give Duncan a call myself." He picked up his coffee mug. "Thanks, Pa," he said, nodding his head in gratitude.
"No worries, Son," Billy replied casually.

"One day, you two are going to show a smidge of excitement," Ally said, throwing her hands up in the air. Ben glanced at Billy and they both chuckled before Ben made his way to the office to make the call.

"Excited by what?" asked a voice behind Ally. She spun around to find Detective Hugh standing there.

"Nothing," she said slowly.

"You're lying, Mom," Hugh said, placing his hands on his hips.

"Come on, I need help with breakfast," Ally said, trying to change the subject. "No one can make pancakes quite like you, Oh Great Glorious Hugh."

"You know that I am not going to let this drop, Mom."

Ally sighed. "I know. But can I at least have a cup of tea first, before your interrogation begins?"

Hugh playfully stroked his chin and he paused to increase the suspense. "Just this once then," he said as he started to get things out for breakfast. Ally rolled her eyes, wondering how long she could delay the conversation. At least there was the distraction of everyone else, she thought.

Billy sat smugly and watched the dramatics in front of him. "I choose first pancake! I've earnt it!" Billy announced, adding yet more fuel to

Hugh's curiosity.

"How have you earnt it?" Hugh turned around to face Billy and then Ally.

Ally slapped her hand against her forehead. "I am going up for a shower," she declared quickly, trying to find an exit from this situation.

Billy began to laugh. "What's so funny? I don't get it?" Hugh said as his head darted from Billy to Ally, and back again. Ally waved her hand dismissively. "He'll explain," she said as she hurriedly disappeared upstairs.

Hugh turned to Billy. "Look, we best make a start on those pancakes," Billy said as he saw John and Sally making their way across to the house. Hugh squinted his eyes as he shifted his detective skills to Billy. "Pancakes," Billy said, pointing towards the cooker.

Hugh huffed. "OK then, I need a pan, a bowl, flour, eggs and milk," he ordered.

"Morning, everyone," Sally said as she stepped through the door.

"Morning, Sally," Hugh greeted over his shoulder. Just then, a pitter-patter of feet was heard coming down the stairs. "Don't start without me," Molly shouted as she jumped in next to Billy.

"Yes! Pancakes!" Aden cried as he ran over to Hugh. Ally arrived, pinned up her wet hair and joined them too.

"Good morning," said John said with a cheeky smile.
"You are very awake for lunch time," Ally replied with a wink.

Ally began to set the table. "So, Miss...or should I say Mrs? What's the first job on the list?" John asked.
"I guess we should start out the back and clear everything away there?" Ally looked up as she placed the plates down.
"OK, while you guys are doing that, I will make a start. Shout me when the food is ready." John walked across the living room and reached for the door handle but as he glanced through the glass, his reflection showed an expression of confusion.

"Very funny, Ally," John said as he re-entered the kitchen.
Ally paused. "What's funny?" she inquired.
"Asking us to tidy up out the back there," John said, shaking his head as he took a seat at the table.
"Is it really that bad?" Ally looked shocked.
"It's worse," replied John, mirroring her expression. "Go and look for yourself."
Ally placed down the glasses and she went to investigate. Everywhere was pristinely clean, like nothing had ever gone on the night before.

Ally marched back into the kitchen. "Did you do that?" she asked as she looked at Sally and John. But they shook their heads. "Billy?"
Billy turned around from the cooker. "Not me," he shrugged.
Ben reappeared from the office. "Did you clean up outside?" Ally asked, now becoming frustrated.
"No, I was asleep next to you," he replied.
"Well, it can't have been Jane. She could barely walk by the end of the night."
"Does it really matter?" queried John. "That's one job to cross off your list."
"That was the only job on my list," Ally said, taking a seat.

Ally's mind spun as Hugh placed the first pancake in front of her. She remained a little dazed as Billy sat down next to her. He took advantage of her state and cheekily slid her plate over so that it was in front of him instead. Ally's attention was then drawn to Jane hobbling across to the house. "Yes! Hugh's pancakes. Just what I need," Jane said as she entered the house and breathed in the smell.
"Did you tidy up outside?" Ally questioned.
"Not guilty," said Jane, holding up her hands.

Ally shook her head. "How odd," she muttered to herself. Hugh attempted, a second time, to put a pancake in front of Ally. And she managed to begin eating this time, before Billy swiped it again.

"Well then, maybe we should be making tracks after breakfast, so we get back before sunset," Sally suggested, looking at John.

"Good idea," he agreed.

The front door then opened again, and Bill stepped through, followed by Helen. "Well, everyone. We are going to hit the highway," Bill said, walking around to Ally. She stood up to give him a hug and then Helen, with a mouthful of pancake. Ally began to motion with her hands and chew rapidly. "Is that a new language you're creating there?" joked Jane, as they all watched the charades.

Ally gulped and took a breath. "Don't be strangers," she said lovingly. "You are welcome here anytime."

"We promise, that on our next adventure, our route will include a visit here," Helen stated. "Is your mum up by the way?" she inquired.

"No, not yet," Ally replied apologetically.

"No problem. Please let her know that I said 'bye' and thank her for all her help with the food."

"Of course," Ally said, giving Helen another hug. Helen and Bill waved their goodbyes and disappeared outside. Everyone listened to the sound of their tyres crunching down the driveway.

Ben looked out of the kitchen window to see Tom and Chad pull their trailer in front of the house and head across. Tom entered first and Chad followed on behind. "Good game?" asked Ben.

Tom raised his eyebrows as Chad entered. "I best be getting back to work seeing as Tom has taken everything I own," groaned Chad as he pinched a pancake and ate it whole.

Ben and Tom began to laugh. "You'll never learn," smirked Ben as he stood up to shake their hands. "I'm sure I'll see you soon, Buddy," Ben said to Tom. "Thanks for all your help."

"Anytime," Tom said as he did his traditional slap on Ben's back. The men headed back to their truck and beeped the horn loudly as they pulled away.

"Well, if you don't mind. I think I am going to make friends with your sofa and a movie," Jane said. Her body still ached. Molly sat down in Jane's place and she swung her legs excitedly under the table at the anticipation of sinking her teeth into a soft pancake.

"Morning, Jane," they all heard Ally's mum call. She then entered the kitchen, pristine and ready for the day ahead.

"Did you clear up outside?" Ally asked, really wanting the mystery to be solved now.

"Yes, of course," answered her mum. "While you

were all sleeping this morning. Then I headed up to get ready and, tah-dah! Here I am," she said casually.

"Oh," was all Ally could manage, feeling a definite pang of guilt.

"Do you want to go on that adventure today, Aden?" Hugh asked eagerly.

Aden turned to Sally and John, his eyes widening with plea. But Sally gently shook her head. "No, maybe some other time," she answered on Aden's behalf.

Hugh couldn't help feeling a little deflated.

"I was kind of hoping that we could test out that new horse of mine?" Ally suggested, keeping her eyes down. She felt the table wiggle from Hugh's excitement.

"What? Do you mean we all get to go out together?" Molly spluttered, her mouth full of pancake.

Ally looked across at Ben. "That sounds like a good plan to me," he approved.

"Well, then that's what we shall do," Ally said, but now becoming apprehensive at the thought. Ally's mum got back up and took her cup of tea with her to go and join Jane.

Sally sipped the last bit of her coffee. "I think we should really head off now."

Aden let out a sigh of disappointment and John

gave his shoulder a reassuring squeeze. "There will be plenty of other opportunities," he said encouragingly.

Aden reluctantly got up, and Molly pushed her chair away from the table so that she could give him a hug. "We'll see you soon," she whispered and Hugh joined the hug too.

Ally headed over to John and Sally. "We must arrange another holiday sometime," Ally hinted.

"First, you best go and enjoy your honeymoon," replied John.

"Yes, we best get that sorted actually," Ally said, glancing back at Ben. Sally, John and Aden made their way outside and waved their goodbyes as they walked past the kitchen window. Ally began to stack the dishwasher as Hugh and Molly devoured the last of the pancakes. "Shall we go and get Firefly and Red Rock ready?" Molly asked, her eyes bright with excitement.

"Yes," nodded Ben. "We will be with you shortly."

"I'll just be in the paddock, doing some more of that fencing," Billy said as he placed his hat on his head and sunk his hands into his pockets.

"You know, you can just sit and relax," Ally suggested guiltily.

"I'll have plenty of time to do that when I'm old," Billy replied.

"So what does that make you now?" Ally asked in

jest. Billy smirked and shook his head as he walked to the door.

Molly and Hugh rapidly munched on the last mouthfuls of their pancakes. "OK, all done," Molly spluttered, leaping up and dashing over to pull her boots on. Hugh was in hot pursuit, and together, they darted off to the barn.
"At what age do you think they'll get bored of doing that?" Ally asked as she placed the last few plates in the dish washer.
"If they are anything like me, then never," said Ben, pretending to leap up and rush to get his boots and hat on too.
Ally shook her head. "What have I become a part of?" she questioned cheekily.
Ben paused. "In true tradition," he said, pulling a pair of boots and a hat from behind the office door. "I think you'll find these fit you quite nicely."
Ally eagerly slipped on the pair of cowgirl boots and her new hat. "How do I look?" she said, striking a pose.
"Ready to help with the chores," laughed Ben.
Ally's face dropped as she took her coat off the peg.

Ally and Ben stepped out onto the front porch, and Ben took her hand as they ambled over to the Barn. "Another beautiful day," observed Ally, looking up at the blue sky.

The closer they got, the more they could hear the echo of Hugh and Molly's voices, and the slamming of stable doors. "I think they may be slightly excited," Ben said with a huge grin.
"I hope Wildfire doesn't live up to his name," Ally remarked as the realisation of riding again dawned on her.
"I would only put you on a horse that I could guarantee you'd be safe on," he said protectively.
"I don't want anything to happen to you." Ally's heartbeat slowed as she held onto the trust that she had in Ben.

As they stepped into the barn, they found that Molly had already lined Red Rock up to the hay bales and was climbing on. Hugh followed.
"We're ready!" they shouted excitedly.
"Well, just give us a minute to catch up with you whirlwind Tasmanian Devils," Ally said as she and Ben disappeared into the tack room to get their saddles and bridles. Ben went to take Wildfire out of his stable and helped Ally start to tack him up. He watched the worried look on Ally's face deepen. "We will take it nice and steady," Ben whispered. Ally swallowed nervously and checked the girth for the fifteenth time. Ben gently guided Wildfire over to the bales of hay and Ally climbed up. She slowly placed her first foot in the stirrup. "All ready for you," Ben said, standing at the other side. Ally took in a deep breath and swung her leg

over, holding tightly to the saddle horn. "Just you wait here," Ben said. Molly and Hugh glanced across at each other but stayed silent. Their excitement was trying to burst out, but they pursed their lips together, trying to contain it.

Ben put the saddle and bridle on his horse. He slipped his foot in the stirrup, and expertly swung up on top. "You make it look so easy," Ally said with a hint of jealousy in her voice. "Well, sometimes I think I am better on these four feet than my own two," he said softly as he rode across to Ally's side. "Right then, you two. Let's head through the gate and up the hill. There is something I would like to show you." Hugh and Molly turned their horses and began to make their way out of the barn. "Ready?" Ben asked quietly as he started to walk. Ally's horse began to follow.
"I don't remember it being as wobbly as this," Ally said as the horse took each step.
"You'll find your rhythm. You just need to relax, and maybe take a breath every once in a while," Ben said, trying to lighten the atmosphere.
"Easy for you to say," Ally huffed as they all continued on their way. Billy was already standing by the gate, holding it open. He tipped his hat as Hugh and Molly rode through.
"Have a nice ride," he said.

"See you in a while," Ben called out as he made sure to keep his horse close to Ally. Billy glanced at Ally as he closed the gate behind them, whose face was now a new shade of white. But, Ally slowly started to loosen her grip on the saddle horn. "Why do you always have to be right?" she sighed. It was true - the more she relaxed, the less unstable she felt. Ben remained quiet as he watched Hugh and Molly stride out as if they had been riding their whole life.

Hugh and Molly marched on ahead. When they reached the top, they both gasped at the view, a beautiful expanse before them. They looked at the valley below and the river flowing at the bottom, at the forest and the rolling green land hugging the sides. They both sat in silence for a moment as they absorbed the closest thing they had ever seen to perfection. Molly was the first to speak. "I will never get used to how amazing this place is." Hugh could only shake his head in awe and agreement. They heard the horse's hooves get louder as Ben and Ally rode up alongside them.

"What is this place?!" Ally cried out as her mouth dropped open. Molly, Hugh and Ben glanced at each other with satisfaction. "This is our home," Ben said simply as his gaze drifted lazily across the land.

"Well, only up to the river," explained Hugh. "The land on the other side belongs to someone else." Ben let the silence linger a little longer and Ally winked across at him. "Not quite, Hugh," he teased. "All of this is our home."
Hugh spun around in his saddle so that he was now sitting backwards on his horse. "What?!" Ben broke into a beaming smile. "See that tree line on the horizon?" he asked, pointing his finger. Hugh spun back around to look and Molly squinted her eyes too. "Yes," they both said together. "Well, our home goes all the way up to those trees."

"But you said the river," Hugh said, feeling frustrated at the thought of missing out on more countryside to explore.
Ben noticed his change in mood. "Hey, hey," he said. "It wasn't until this morning that Grandpa Billy gave it to us as a gift," Ben replied.
"That makes more sense," Molly mused.
"So, you mean all the way over there," cried Hugh, still staring intensely at the far-reaching view.
Ben nodded as he reached across to take hold of Ally's hand. "Yes, Hugh," Ben confirmed. "We have been given the greatest gift of all - the gift of time. Time is something so precious, but something that people waste the most. You can never buy or get more time. We all have a set

185

amount, yet we don't know how much we have got until it's too late. This land means that we have the freedom to choose how we want to spend our time, but it is our responsibility to spend it wisely." They all sat for a moment as they watched the land subtly change. A leaf blew through the air and the water rolled over a rock - the land ever-moving in synchronicity.

"Last one to the river is a lobster!" Hugh shouted as he nudged his horse to move. "Wait! No fair. You got a head start," groaned Molly as she kicked on and Red Rock rolled up into a canter. They both weaved their way down towards the river. Hugh and Firefly were getting ever quicker.

Ally grabbed hold of the saddle horn again and her knuckles turned white. "Please say we don't have to go that fast downhill!" she pleaded. "I think we can let them race on ahead," Ben said reassuringly. "We can take our time and enjoy more of the view. We will all end up at the same place in the end." Ben gently started to walk forwards, still holding onto Ally's hand and Wildfire obediently followed.

"I still can't quite believe this is real," Ally breathed as Ben easily navigated the path. "You and me both. But I'm not complaining. I do know the responsibility that comes with it though.

All the creatures, the land and the water is under our care now. We can either destroy it or protect it, which won't always be so easy," Ben continued.

Ally listened intently. "I understand. God help anyone who tries to destroy it though. They wouldn't survive the telling-off from Hugh!" Ally laughed.

"Or Molly for that matter," Ben added. As the land began to level out and the sound of the running water grew louder, Ally felt a new sense of calmness grow, like a seed inside of her.

"Can we cross over?" Hugh asked eagerly, already standing in the water up to Firefly's knees.

"Yes, but go carefully," Ben said as he continued to help Ally. But he watched her confidence begin to grow with each step. Hugh ploughed on ahead but Molly navigated Red Rock more delicately through the river. They both stopped when they reached the other side, and watched Ally and Ben follow on. "Hey, Mom," called Hugh. "You actually look OK on Wildfire!"

"I'm glad I have your thumbs up, Monkey," replied Ally. "But, I think I will be sticking to a walk for a while."

"Oh, Mom. Where's your sense of adventure?" Hugh asked, flopping back on Firefly's back to look up at the blue sky. But, he suddenly felt a sharp swat of a branch. "Ow!" he cried. "What was that for?". He turned to see Molly, smiling smugly.

"That is the consequence of your words," she said, swatting him again. "Some words hurt, you know."

"Ow! Stop that!" shouted Hugh, trying to grab hold of the branch, but Molly whipped it away too quickly.

Hugh huffed as they all began to ride up the other side of the valley. The anticipation of what lay ahead grew and grew as Hugh and Molly increased the pace. They listened to their breathing get quicker with excitement. As the horse's noses peered over the brow of the valley side, Hugh and Molly gasped and their hands flew to their mouths. Firefly and Red Rock to come to an abrupt stop. Ben called up from below.

'Always be ready to receive'

If you have enjoyed this book, please pass it on or share it with those you know, so that we can continue to spread the wisdom woven into Ally, Ben, Hugh and Molly's story.

Can You Help?

We would love to hear what you thought about the book.

1. Go to Amazon;

2. Type 'Naomi Sharp' into the search box and press enter;

3. Click on the book;

4. Scroll down until you reach the star chart;

5. Click the button and write a review.

Every review received is a wonderful gift each day. Thank you.

With gratitude,

Naomi

8 ABOUT THE AUTHOR

www.naomisharpauthor.com

Naomi began making notes when she was just 10 years old. Still today, she always has a notebook to hand, ready to jot down the next profound thought or idea.

It wasn't until 6 years later that Naomi would write her first book: Living Life With The Glass Half Full. In it, she shares her story of changing life's adversity into lessons learned. No sooner had she finished that book, she was inspired to write her next: A Diary Of Dreams, her first work of fiction. Naomi describes the experience as, 'downloading a story, like a movie was playing in front of me and I was writing down what was happening, moment by moment.'

Naomi's passion to inspire people to heal and find hope and happiness continues to grow. So, she continues to write. She feels that storytelling is an incredible way to pass on wisdom and life's truths.

Naomi trained as an Occupational Therapist but became fascinated by horses. In particular, their ability to help people heal, not only physically, but also mentally and emotionally. Her passion for understanding how we can help our bodies to heal and our dreams to become reality has brought some breath taking experiences into her life. She has had the opportunity to meet some incredible people and visit some memorable places.

During the day, Naomi also runs her therapy centre for individuals with a mental, physical or emotional disability. These people can come and spend time with horses, and celebrate what makes them unique.

9 OTHER BOOKS BY NAOMI SHARP

A Diary Of Dreams (Universal Series Book 1)

A journey to remembering that dreams can come true.

Finding love and happiness, following the death of a family member, by living your dreams. Hugh watched his mom's happiness dissolve away as a dark depression took hold. All Ally could see was the new absence in her life, a love that was no longer there. Hugh dreamed of his mom finding her happiness, falling in love and rediscovering the magic of life. He visualised her allowing the lost love to transform as they embarked on a new chapter in life. Hugh decided to create a map of dreams, a vision board, of all the things he wanted to happen in his life. This resulted in an adventure that took him and Ally to meet the people they needed to meet, and visit the places they needed to go. It took them towards dreams they wanted to experience, and they discovered how truly magical life could be. This book will help to inspire you to plan for and dream of the life you truly desire. It will empower women and children to have the courage to follow their heart's desires, thus enabling their ambitions in life to flourish. An incredible story of how family, dreams and love can help you achieve anything you want.

A Locket of Love (Universal Series Book 2)

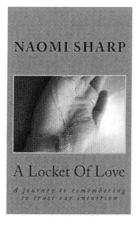

A journey to remembering to follow our intuition.

As Nana O waited for Molly to arrive, she sat in her usual chair by the fire. She twiddled her thumbs and began to think about the story that she was going to tell, about a locket and the secret it holds.

Molly arrived, feeling awkward and shuffling her feet. She didn't want to be there, but sat down on the stool in front of Nana O anyway. She quickly became captivated as the story began to unfold. Nana O told Molly about a single locket that held a secret. That secret would help Molly to remember and understand how to follow her own intuition. Molly begins to follow it, day by day, and her life begins to transform. She slowly becomes the person she was meant to be. She is closely followed, on her journey, by her two best friends, Layla and Dillon, who are always there, supporting her along the way.

Throughout the book there are golden nuggets of wisdom which will help you to remember life truths that may have been forgotten. This is the second book in the universal series, looking at the law of oneness.

A Mirror of Miracles (Universal Series Book 3)

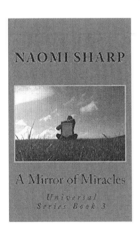

A journey to remembering the power of self-image.

Hugh paces the living room, waiting for the arrival of Molly. Butterflies swirl around in his stomach. As the truck pulls up in front of the house, Hugh leaps into action and sprints to the front door. Molly steps out of the truck and Hugh heads straight for her. Molly flings her arms around him as Hugh whispers, 'Welcome home.'

As Molly and Hugh stand in front of the mirror,

Billy begins to reveal the next of life's truths. This starts a life changing adventure as they begin to understand and practise this new truth.

Molly's parents announce they are heading back to England early, leaving Molly with Ally, Ben and Hugh. None of them realise what is waiting for them all just around the next corner, causing life to never be the same again.

A Feather of Faith (Universal Series Book 4)

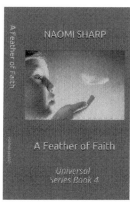

The moment you are consumed by fear, a spark of faith ignites, helping the path that needs to be taken to become clear.

A journey to remembering that the tests we go through in life are there to strengthen us to follow our dreams.

As Molly comes to terms with the news, she lowers the letter and knows what needs to be done, and she prepares herself to unpick the threads of her old life. Nana O's star shines brightly and helps Molly to find her way through her darkest time. Ally organises the plane tickets but feels numb from the events that have occurred. She packs her bags once more to return to the land she wishes she could forget. Ally is forced to step back into a life that she not long ago fled from, yet this time, as she crosses over the threshold, back through her front door, she feels the touch of another hand giving her the strength to continue on.

Hugh spreads the map across the kitchen table. They all watch his finger trace the road they need to travel, to make a wish at the waterfalls and find their luck once more. As they meet new and old friends, each person helps them to remember one of life's truth's. Yet will it be enough or will their fear and heartache stop all their dreams coming true?

Living Life With The Glass Half Full

An inspiring true story of how a young girl chooses to learn from life's adversity with the help of horses. She travels to Ireland, France and America to understand how to live a better, happier life, and to understand what it truly means to heal. The story follows her from her younger days, causing mischief in nursery, through to the frustration of being dyslexic in school. This leads to her whole world being turned around with a profound realisation. All the while, different horses are guiding her path with their constant friendship and companionship. They continually highlight some of the facts of life that Naomi has picked up along the way. The book includes a bonus feature for your own personal development. It provides ways for you to analyse your life's problems and turn them into positives, with surprising ease. It encourages you to work through your own challenges by changing your perceptions on how you view life and adversity. This book provides a true account of how the adventure of life is more about using your lessons to help dreams become reality, rather than allowing adversity to become your future.

40 Days Transforming Your Life

Do you feel your back is up against the wall? Help has arrived!
In this 'how-to' book, you will discover a *40 day process* that will help you and your life to transform. You will be taken from a place of despair to a place where dreams come true.

You won't be doing this journey alone though. Every day, there is a short chapter which will look at what the day ahead has in store, as you move up and down the emotional scale. In this 'how-to' book, you will explore what it means to change from the inside out. It will provide pearls of wisdom, to keep you inspired and motivated to move forwards.

Aspects included in 40 Days Transforming Your Life:

~ Letting go of past experiences;
~ Loving yourself and your strengths;
~ Learning to set a goal or dream;
~ Setting up your routine for success;
~ Celebrating your achievements;
~ Worry no longer being part of your day.

40 Days Transforming Your Life, by Naomi Sharp, will help you develop a simple but sustainable routine to reaching your goals, transforming your life, and living your dreams.

Printed in Great Britain
by Amazon

36720638R00123